Within the Tides

Joseph Conrad

Within the Tides

Joseph Conrad

© 1st World Library – Literary Society, 2004
PO Box 2211
Fairfield, IA 52556
www.1stworldlibrary.org
First Edition

LCCN: 2004091231

Softcover ISBN: 1-59540-669-7
Hardcover ISBN: 1-4218-0969-9
eBook ISBN: 1-59540-769-3

Purchase *"Within the Tides"*
as a traditional bound book at:
www.1stWorldLibrary.org/purchase.asp?ISBN=1-59540-669-7

1st World Library Literary Society is a nonprofit
organization dedicated to promoting literacy by:

- Creating a free internet library accessible from any
  computer worldwide.
- Hosting writing competitions and offering book
  publishing scholarships.

Readers interested in supporting literacy
through sponsorship, donations or
membership please contact:
literacy@1stworldlibrary.org
Check us out at: www.1stworldlibrary.ORG
and start downloading free ebooks today.

Within the Tides
contributed by the Charles Family
in support of
1st World Library Literary Society

CONTENTS

THE PLANTER OF MALATA

CHAPTER I

In the private editorial office of the principal newspaper in a great colonial city two men were talking. They were both young. The stouter of the two, fair, and with more of an urban look about him, was the editor and part-owner of the important newspaper.

The other's name was Renouard. That he was exercised in his mind about something was evident on his fine bronzed face. He was a lean, lounging, active man. The journalist continued the conversation.

"And so you were dining yesterday at old Dunster's."

He used the word old not in the endearing sense in which it is sometimes applied to intimates, but as a matter of sober fact. The Dunster in question was old. He had been an eminent colonial statesman, but had now retired from active politics after a tour in Europe and a lengthy stay in England, during which he had had a very good press indeed. The colony was proud of him.

"Yes. I dined there," said Renouard. "Young Dunster asked me just as I was going out of his office. It seemed to be like a sudden thought. And yet I can't help suspecting some purpose behind it. He was very pressing. He swore that his uncle would be very pleased to see me. Said his uncle had mentioned lately that the granting to me of the Malata concession was the last act of his official life."

"Very touching. The old boy sentimentalises over the past now and then."

"I really don't know why I accepted," continued the other. "Sentiment does not move me very easily. Old Dunster was civil to me of course, but he did not even inquire how I was getting on with my silk plants. Forgot there was such a thing probably. I must say there were more people there than I expected to meet. Quite a big party."

"I was asked," remarked the newspaper man. "Only I couldn't go. But when did you arrive from Malata?"

"I arrived yesterday at daylight. I am anchored out there in the bay - off Garden Point. I was in Dunster's office before he had finished reading his letters. Have you ever seen young Dunster reading his letters? I had a glimpse of him through the open door. He holds the paper in both hands, hunches his shoulders up to his ugly ears, and brings his long nose and his thick lips on to it like a sucking apparatus. A commercial monster."

"Here we don't consider him a monster," said the newspaper man looking at his visitor thoughtfully.

"Probably not. You are used to see his face and to see other faces. I don't know how it is that, when I come to town, the appearance of the people in the street strike me with such force. They seem so awfully expressive."

"And not charming."

"Well - no. Not as a rule. The effect is forcible without being clear. . . . I know that you think it's because of my solitary manner of life away there."

"Yes. I do think so. It is demoralising. You don't see any one for months at a stretch. You're leading an unhealthy life."

The other hardly smiled and murmured the admission that true enough it was a good eleven months since he had been in town last.

"You see," insisted the other. "Solitude works like a sort of poison. And then you perceive suggestions in faces - mysterious and forcible, that no sound man would be bothered with. Of course you do."

Geoffrey Renouard did not tell his journalist friend that the suggestions of his own face, the face of a friend, bothered him as much as the others. He detected a degrading quality in the touches of age which every day adds to a human countenance. They moved and disturbed him, like the signs of a horrible inward travail which was frightfully apparent to the fresh eye he had brought from his isolation in Malata, where he had settled after five strenuous years of adventure and exploration.

"It's a fact," he said, "that when I am at home in Malata I see no one consciously. I take the plantation boys for granted."

"Well, and we here take the people in the streets for granted. And that's sanity."

The visitor said nothing to this for fear of engaging a discussion. What he had come to seek in the editorial office was not controversy, but information. Yet somehow he hesitated to approach the subject. Solitary life makes a man reticent in respect of anything in the nature of gossip, which those to whom chatting about their kind is an everyday exercise regard as the commonest use of speech.

"You very busy?" he asked.

The Editor making red marks on a long slip of printed paper threw the pencil down.

"No. I am done. Social paragraphs. This office is the place where everything is known about everybody - including even a great deal of nobodies. Queer fellows drift in and out of this room. Waifs and strays from home, from up-country, from the Pacific. And, by the way, last time you were here you picked up one of that sort for your assistant - didn't you?"

"I engaged an assistant only to stop your preaching about the evils of solitude," said Renouard hastily; and the pressman laughed at the half-resentful tone. His laugh was not very loud, but his plump person shook all over. He was aware that his younger friend's deference to his advice was based only on an imperfect belief in his wisdom - or his sagacity. But it was he who had first helped Renouard in his plans of exploration: the five-years' programme of scientific adventure, of work, of danger and endurance, carried out with such distinction and rewarded modestly with the lease of Malata island by the frugal colonial government. And this reward, too, had been due to the journalist's advocacy with word and pen - for he was an influential man in the community. Doubting very much if Renouard really liked him, he was himself without great sympathy for a certain side of that man which he could not quite make out. He only felt it obscurely to be his real personality - the true - and, perhaps, the absurd. As, for instance, in that case of the assistant. Renouard had given way to the arguments of his friend and backer - the argument against the unwholesome effect of solitude, the argument for the safety of companionship even if quarrelsome. Very well. In this docility he was sensible and even likeable. But what did he do next? Instead of taking counsel as to the choice with his old backer and friend, and a man, besides, knowing everybody employed and unemployed on the pavements of the town, this extraordinary Renouard suddenly and almost surreptitiously picked up a fellow - God knows who - and sailed away with him back to Malata in a hurry; a proceeding obviously rash and at the same time not quite straight. That was the sort of thing. The secretly unforgiving journalist laughed a little longer and then ceased to shake all over.

"Oh, yes. About that assistant of yours. . . ."

"What about him," said Renouard, after waiting a while, with a shadow of uneasiness on his face.

"Have you nothing to tell me of him?"

"Nothing except. . . ." Incipient grimness vanished out of Renouard's aspect and his voice, while he hesitated as if reflecting seriously before he changed his mind.

"No. Nothing whatever."

"You haven't brought him along with you by chance - for a change."

The Planter of Malata stared, then shook his head, and finally murmured carelessly: "I think he's very well where he is. But I wish you could tell me why young Dunster insisted so much on my dining with his uncle last night. Everybody knows I am not a society man."

The Editor exclaimed at so much modesty. Didn't his friend know that he was their one and only explorer - that he was the man experimenting with the silk plant.

"Still, that doesn't tell me why I was invited yesterday. For young Dunster never thought of this civility before. . . ."

"Our Willie," said the popular journalist, "never does anything without a purpose, that's a fact."

"And to his uncle's house too!"

"He lives there."

"Yes. But he might have given me a feed somewhere else. The extraordinary part is that the old man did not seem to have anything special to say. He smiled kindly on me once or twice, and that was all. It was quite a party, sixteen people."

The Editor then, after expressing his regret that he had not been able to come, wanted to know if the party had been entertaining.

Joseph Conrad

Renouard regretted that his friend had not been there. Being a man whose business or at least whose profession was to know everything that went on in this part of the globe, he could probably have told him something of some people lately arrived from home, who were amongst the guests. Young Dunster (Willie), with his large shirt-front and streaks of white skin shining unpleasantly through the thin black hair plastered over the top of his head, bore down on him and introduced him to that party, as if he had been a trained dog or a child phenomenon. Decidedly, he said, he disliked Willie-one of these large oppressive men.

A silence fell, and it was as if Renouard were not going to say anything more when, suddenly, he came out with the real object of his visit to the editorial room.

"They looked to me like people under a spell."

The Editor gazed at him appreciatively, thinking that, whether the effect of solitude or not, this was a proof of a sensitive perception of the expression of faces.

"You omitted to tell me their name, but I can make a guess. You mean Professor Moorsom, his daughter and sister - don't you?"

Renouard assented. Yes, a white-haired lady. But from his silence, with his eyes fixed, yet avoiding his friend, it was easy to guess that it was not in the white-haired lady that he was interested.

"Upon my word," he said, recovering his usual bearing. "It looks to me as if I had been asked there only for the daughter to talk to me."

He did not conceal that he had been greatly struck by her appearance. Nobody could have helped being impressed. She was different from everybody else in that house, and it was not only the effect of her London clothes. He did not take her down to dinner. Willie did that. It was afterwards, on the terrace. . . .

The evening was delightfully calm. He was sitting apart and alone, and wishing himself somewhere else - on board the schooner for choice, with the dinner-harness off. He hadn't exchanged forty words altogether during the evening with the other guests. He saw her suddenly all by herself coming towards him along the dimly lighted terrace, quite from a distance.

She was tall and supple, carrying nobly on her straight body a head of a character which to him appeared peculiar, something - well - pagan, crowned with a great wealth of hair. He had been about to rise, but her decided approach caused him to remain on the seat. He had not looked much at her that evening. He had not that freedom of gaze acquired by the habit of society and the frequent meetings with strangers. It was not shyness, but the reserve of a man not used to the world and to the practice of covert staring, with careless curiosity. All he had captured by his first, keen, instantly lowered, glance was the impression that her hair was magnificently red and her eyes very black. It was a troubling effect, but it had been evanescent; he had forgotten it almost till very unexpectedly he saw her coming down the terrace slow and eager, as if she were restraining herself, and with a rhythmic upward undulation of her whole figure. The light from an open window fell across her path, and suddenly all that mass of arranged hair appeared incandescent, chiselled and fluid, with the daring suggestion of a helmet of

Joseph Conrad

burnished copper and the flowing lines of molten metal. It kindled in him an astonished admiration. But he said nothing of it to his friend the Editor. Neither did he tell him that her approach woke up in his brain the image of love's infinite grace and the sense of the inexhaustible joy that lives in beauty. No! What he imparted to the Editor were no emotions, but mere facts conveyed in a deliberate voice and in uninspired words.

"That young lady came and sat down by me. She said: 'Are you French, Mr. Renouard?'"

He had breathed a whiff of perfume of which he said nothing either-of some perfume he did not know. Her voice was low and distinct. Her shoulders and her bare arms gleamed with an extraordinary splendour, and when she advanced her head into the light he saw the admirable contour of the face, the straight fine nose with delicate nostrils, the exquisite crimson brushstroke of the lips on this oval without colour. The expression of the eyes was lost in a shadowy mysterious play of jet and silver, stirring under the red coppery gold of the hair as though she had been a being made of ivory and precious metals changed into living tissue.

". . . I told her my people were living in Canada, but that I was brought up in England before coming out here. I can't imagine what interest she could have in my history."

"And you complain of her interest?"

The accent of the all-knowing journalist seemed to jar on the Planter of Malata.

"No!" he said, in a deadened voice that was almost sullen. But after a short silence he went on. "Very extraordinary. I told her I came out to wander at large in the world when I was nineteen, almost directly after I left school. It seems that her late brother was in the same school a couple of years before me. She wanted me to tell her what I did at first when I came out here; what other men found to do when they came out - where they went, what was likely to happen to them - as if I could guess and foretell from my experience the fates of men who come out here with a hundred different projects, for hundreds of different reasons – for no reason but restlessness - who come, and go, and disappear! Preposterous. She seemed to want to hear their histories. I told her that most of them were not worth telling."

The distinguished journalist leaning on his elbow, his head resting against the knuckles of his left hand, listened with great attention, but gave no sign of that surprise which Renouard, pausing, seemed to expect.

"You know something," the latter said brusquely. The all-knowing man moved his head slightly and said, "Yes. But go on."

"It's just this. There is no more to it. I found myself talking to her of my adventures, of my early days. It couldn't possibly have interested her. Really," he cried, "this is most extraordinary. Those people have something on their minds. We sat in the light of the window, and her father prowled about the terrace, with his hands behind his back and his head drooping. The white-haired lady came to the dining-room window twice - to look at us I am certain. The other guests began to go away - and still we sat there. Apparently these people are staying with the Dunsters. It was old Mrs. Dunster who put an end to the thing. The father and the aunt circled about as if they were afraid of interfering with the girl. Then she got up all at once, gave me her hand, and said she hoped she would see me again."

While he was speaking Renouard saw again the sway of her figure in a movement of grace and strength - felt the pressure of her hand - heard the last accents of the deep murmur that came from her throat so white in the light of the window, and remembered the black rays of her steady eyes passing off his face when she turned away. He remembered all this visually, and it was not exactly pleasurable. It was rather startling like the discovery of a new faculty in himself. There are faculties one would rather do without - such, for instance, as seeing through a stone wall or remembering a person with this uncanny vividness. And what about those two people belonging to her with their air of expectant solicitude! Really, those figures from home got in front of one. In fact, their persistence in getting between him and the solid forms of the everyday material world had driven Renouard to call on his friend at the office. He hoped that a little common, gossipy information would lay the ghost of that unexpected dinner-party. Of course the proper person to go to would have been young Dunster, but, he couldn't stand Willie Dunster - not at any price.

In the pause the Editor had changed his attitude, faced his desk, and smiled a faint knowing smile.

"Striking girl - eh?" he said.

The incongruity of the word was enough to make one

jump out of the chair. Striking! That girl striking! Stri !
But Renouard restrained his feelings. His friend was
not a person to give oneself away to. And, after all, this
sort of speech was what he had come there to hear. As,
however, he had made a movement he re-settled
himself comfortably and said, with very creditable
indifference, that yes - she was, rather. Especially
amongst a lot of over-dressed frumps. There wasn't
one woman under forty there.

"Is that the way to speak of the cream of our society;
the 'top of the basket,' as the French say," the Editor
remonstrated with mock indignation. "You aren't
moderate in your expressions - you know."

"I express myself very little," interjected Renouard
seriously.

"I will tell you what you are. You are a fellow that
doesn't count the cost. Of course you are safe with me,
but will you never learn. . . ."

"What struck me most," interrupted the other, "is that
she should pick me out for such a long conversation."

"That's perhaps because you were the most remarkable
of the men there."

Renouard shook his head.

"This shot doesn't seem to me to hit the mark," he said
calmly. "Try again."

"Don't you believe me? Oh, you modest creature.
Well, let me assure you that under ordinary
circumstances it would have been a good shot. You are

Joseph Conrad

sufficiently remarkable. But you seem a pretty acute customer too. The circumstances are extraordinary. By Jove they are!"

He mused. After a time the Planter of Malata dropped a negligent -

"And you know them."

"And I know them," assented the all-knowing Editor, soberly, as though the occasion were too special for a display of professional vanity; a vanity so well known to Renouard that its absence augmented his wonder and almost made him uneasy as if portending bad news of some sort.

"You have met those people?" he asked.

"No. I was to have met them last night, but I had to send an apology to Willie in the morning. It was then that he had the bright idea to invite you to fill the place, from a muddled notion that you could be of use. Willie is stupid sometimes. For it is clear that you are the last man able to help."

"How on earth do I come to be mixed up in this - whatever it is?" Renouard's voice was slightly altered by nervous irritation. "I only arrived here yesterday morning."

CHAPTER II

His friend the Editor turned to him squarely. "Willie took me into consultation, and since he seems to have let you in I may just as well tell you what is up. I shall try to be as short as I can. But in confidence - mind!"

He waited. Renouard, his uneasiness growing on him unreasonably, assented by a nod, and the other lost no time in beginning. Professor Moorsom - physicist and philosopher - fine head of white hair, to judge from the photographs - plenty of brains in the head too - all these famous books - surely even Renouard would know. . . .

Renouard muttered moodily that it wasn't his sort of reading, and his friend hastened to assure him earnestly that neither was it his sort - except as a matter of business and duty, for the literary page of that newspaper which was his property (and the pride of his life). The only literary newspaper in the Antipodes could not ignore the fashionable philosopher of the age. Not that anybody read Moorsom at the Antipodes, but everybody had heard of him - women, children, dock labourers, cabmen. The only person (besides himself) who had read Moorsom, as far as he knew, was old Dunster, who used to call himself a Moorsomian (or was it Moorsomite) years and years ago, long before Moorsom had worked himself up into

Joseph Conrad

the great swell he was now, in every way. . . . Socially too. Quite the fashion in the highest world.

Renouard listened with profoundly concealed attention. "A charlatan," he muttered languidly.

"Well - no. I should say not. I shouldn't wonder though if most of his writing had been done with his tongue in his cheek. Of course. That's to be expected. I tell you what: the only really honest writing is to be found in newspapers and nowhere else - and don't you forget it."

The Editor paused with a basilisk stare till Renouard had conceded a casual: "I dare say," and only then went on to explain that old Dunster, during his European tour, had been made rather a lion of in London, where he stayed with the Moorsoms - he meant the father and the girl. The professor had been a widower for a long time.

"She doesn't look just a girl," muttered Renouard. The other agreed. Very likely not. Had been playing the London hostess to tip-top people ever since she put her hair up, probably.

"I don't expect to see any girlish bloom on her when I do have the privilege," he continued. "Those people are staying with the Dunster's incog., in a manner, you understand - something like royalties. They don't deceive anybody, but they want to be left to themselves. We have even kept them out of the paper - to oblige old Dunster. But we shall put your arrival in - our local celebrity."

"Heavens!"

"Yes. Mr. G. Renouard, the explorer, whose indomitable energy, etc., and who is now working for the prosperity of our country in another way on his Malata plantation . . . And, by the by, how's the silk plant - flourishing?"

"Yes."

"Did you bring any fibre?"

"Schooner-full."

"I see. To be transhipped to Liverpool for experimental manufacture, eh? Eminent capitalists at home very much interested, aren't they?"

"They are."

A silence fell. Then the Editor uttered slowly - "You will be a rich man some day."

Renouard's face did not betray his opinion of that confident prophecy. He didn't say anything till his friend suggested in the same meditative voice -

"You ought to interest Moorsom in the affair too - since Willie has let you in."

"A philosopher!"

"I suppose he isn't above making a bit of money. And he may be clever at it for all you know. I have a notion that he's a fairly practical old cove. . . . Anyhow," and here the tone of the speaker took on a tinge of respect, "he has made philosophy pay."

Renouard raised his eyes, repressed an impulse to jump up, and got out of the arm-chair slowly. "It isn't perhaps a bad idea," he said. "I'll have to call there in any case."

He wondered whether he had managed to keep his voice steady, its tone unconcerned enough; for his emotion was strong though it had nothing to do with the business aspect of this suggestion. He moved in the room in vague preparation for departure, when he heard a soft laugh. He spun about quickly with a frown, but the Editor was not laughing at him. He was chuckling across the big desk at the wall: a preliminary of some speech for which Renouard, recalled to himself, waited silent and mistrustful.

"No! You would never guess! No one would ever guess what these people are after. Willie's eyes bulged out when he came to me with the tale."

"They always do," remarked Renouard with disgust. "He's stupid."

"He was startled. And so was I after he told me. It's a search party. They are out looking for a man. Willie's soft heart's enlisted in the cause."

Renouard repeated: "Looking for a man."

He sat down suddenly as if on purpose to stare. "Did Willie come to you to borrow the lantern," he asked sarcastically, and got up again for no apparent reason.

"What lantern?" snapped the puzzled Editor, and his face darkened with suspicion. "You, Renouard, are always alluding to things that aren't clear to me. If you were in politics, I, as a party journalist, wouldn't trust you further than I could see you. Not an inch further. You are such a sophisticated beggar. Listen: the man is the man Miss Moorsom was engaged to for a year. He couldn't have been a nobody, anyhow. But he doesn't seem to have been very wise. Hard luck for the young lady."

He spoke with feeling. It was clear that what he had to tell appealed to his sentiment. Yet, as an experienced man of the world, he marked his amused wonder. Young man of good family and connections, going everywhere, yet not merely a man about town, but with a foot in the two big F's.

Renouard lounging aimlessly in the room turned round: "And what the devil's that?" he asked faintly.

"Why Fashion and Finance," explained the Editor. "That's how I call it. There are the three R's at the bottom of the social edifice and the two F's on the top. See?"

"Ha! Ha! Excellent! Ha! Ha!" Renouard laughed with stony eyes.

"And you proceed from one set to the other in this democratic age," the Editor went on with unperturbed complacency. "That is if you are clever enough. The only danger is in being too clever. And I think something of the sort happened here. That swell I am speaking of got himself into a mess. Apparently a very ugly mess of a financial character. You will understand that Willie did not go into details with me. They were not imparted to him with very great abundance either. But a bad mess - something of the criminal order. Of course he was innocent. But he had to quit all the same."

"Ha! Ha!" Renouard laughed again abruptly, staring as before. "So there's one more big F in the tale."

"What do you mean?" inquired the Editor quickly, with an air as if his patent were being infringed.

"I mean - Fool."

"No. I wouldn't say that. I wouldn't say that."

"Well - let him be a scoundrel then. What the devil do I care."

"But hold on! You haven't heard the end of the story."

Renouard, his hat on his head already, sat down with the disdainful smile of a man who had discounted the moral of the story. Still he sat down and the Editor swung his revolving chair right round. He was full of unction.

"Imprudent, I should say. In many ways money is as dangerous to handle as gunpowder. You can't be too careful either as to who you are working with. Anyhow there was a mighty flashy burst up, a sensation, and - his familiar haunts knew him no more. But before he vanished he went to see Miss Moorsom. That very fact argues for his innocence - don't it? What was said between them no man knows - unless the professor had the confidence from his daughter. There couldn't have been much to say. There was nothing for it but to let him go - was there? - for the affair had got into the papers. And perhaps the kindest thing would have been to forget him. Anyway the easiest. Forgiveness would have been more difficult, I fancy, for a young lady of spirit and position drawn into an ugly affair like that. Any ordinary young lady, I mean. Well, the fellow asked nothing better than to be forgotten, only he didn't find it easy to do so himself, because he would write home now and then. Not to any of his friends though. He had no near relations. The professor had been his guardian. No, the poor devil wrote now and then to an old retired butler of his late father, somewhere in the country, forbidding him at the same time to let any one know of his whereabouts. So that worthy old ass would go up and dodge about the Moorsom's town house, perhaps waylay Miss Moorsom's maid, and then would write to 'Master Arthur' that the young lady looked well and happy, or some such cheerful intelligence. I dare say he wanted to be forgotten, but I shouldn't think he was much cheered by the news. What would you say?"

Renouard, his legs stretched out and his chin on his breast, said nothing. A sensation which was not curiosity, but rather a vague nervous anxiety, distinctly unpleasant, like a mysterious symptom of some malady, prevented him from getting up and going away.

"Mixed feelings," the Editor opined. "Many fellows out here receive news from home with mixed feelings. But what will his feelings be when he hears what I am going to tell you now? For we know he has not heard yet. Six months ago a city clerk, just a common drudge of finance, gets himself convicted of a common embezzlement or something of that kind. Then seeing he's in for a long sentence he thinks of making his conscience comfortable, and makes a clean breast of an old story of tampered with, or else suppressed, documents, a story which clears altogether the honesty of our ruined gentleman. That embezzling fellow was in a position to know, having been employed by the firm before the smash. There was no doubt about the character being cleared - but where the cleared man was nobody could tell. Another sensation in society. And then Miss Moorsom says: 'He will come back to claim me, and I'll marry him.' But he didn't come back. Between you and me I don't think he was much wanted - except by Miss Moorsom. I imagine she's used to have her own way. She grew impatient, and declared that if she knew where the man was she would go to him. But all that could be got out of the old butler was that the last envelope bore the postmark of our beautiful city; and that this was the only address of 'Master Arthur' that he ever had. That and no more. In fact the fellow was at his last gasp - with a bad heart. Miss Moorsom wasn't allowed to see him. She had gone herself into the country to learn what she could, but she had to stay downstairs while the old chap's wife went up to the invalid. She brought down the scrap of intelligence I've told you of. He was already too far gone to be cross-examined on it, and that very night he died. He didn't leave behind him much to go by, did he? Our Willie hinted to me that there had been pretty stormy days in the professor's house, but - here they are. I have a notion she isn't the kind of everyday young lady who may be permitted to gallop about the world all by herself - eh? Well, I think it rather fine of her, but I quite understand that the professor needed all his philosophy under the circumstances. She is his only child now - and brilliant - what? Willie positively spluttered trying to describe her to me; and I could see directly you came in that you had an uncommon experience."

Renouard, with an irritated gesture, tilted his hat more forward on his eyes, as though he were bored. The Editor went on with the remark that to be sure neither he (Renouard) nor yet Willie were much used to meet girls of that remarkable superiority. Willie when learning business with a firm in London, years before, had seen none but boarding-house society, he guessed. As to himself in the good old days, when he trod the glorious flags of Fleet Street, he neither had access to, nor yet would have cared for the swells. Nothing interested him then but parliamentary politics and the oratory of the House of Commons.

He paid to this not very distant past the tribute of a tender, reminiscent smile, and returned to his first idea that for a society girl her action was rather fine. All the same the professor could not be very pleased. The fellow if he was as pure as a lily now was just about as devoid of the goods of the earth. And there were misfortunes, however undeserved, which damaged a man's standing permanently. On the other hand, it was difficult to oppose cynically a noble impulse - not to speak of the great love at the root of it. Ah! Love! And then the lady was quite capable of going off by herself. She was of age, she had money of her own, plenty of pluck too. Moorsom must have concluded that it was more truly paternal, more prudent too, and generally safer all round to let himself be dragged into this chase. The aunt came along for the same reasons. It was given out at home as a trip round the world of the usual kind.

Renouard had risen and remained standing with his heart beating, and strangely affected by this tale, robbed as it was of all glamour by the prosaic personality of the narrator. The Editor added: "I've been asked to help in the search - you know."

Renouard muttered something about an appointment and went out into the street. His inborn sanity could not defend him from a misty creeping jealousy. He thought that obviously no man of that sort could be worthy of such a woman's devoted fidelity. Renouard, however, had lived long enough to reflect that a man's activities, his views, and even his ideas may be very inferior to his character; and moved by a delicate consideration for that splendid girl he tried to think out for the man a character of inward excellence and outward gifts - some extraordinary seduction. But in vain. Fresh from months of solitude and from days at sea, her splendour presented itself to him absolutely unconquerable in its perfection, unless by her own folly. It was easier to suspect her of this than to imagine in the man qualities which would be worthy of her. Easier and less degrading. Because folly may be generous-could be nothing else but generosity in her; whereas to imagine her subjugated by something common was intolerable.

Because of the force of the physical impression he had received from her personality (and such impressions are the real origins of the deepest movements of our soul) this conception of her was even inconceivable. But no Prince Charming has ever lived out of a fairy tale. He doesn't walk the worlds of Fashion and Finance - and with a stumbling gait at that. Generosity. Yes. It was her generosity. But this generosity was altogether regal in its splendour, almost absurd in its lavishness - or, perhaps, divine.

In the evening, on board his schooner, sitting on the rail, his arms folded on his breast and his eyes fixed on the deck, he let the darkness catch him unawares in the midst of a meditation on the mechanism of sentiment and the springs of passion. And all the time he had an abiding consciousness of her bodily presence. The effect on his senses had been so penetrating that in the middle of the night, rousing up suddenly, wide-eyed in the darkness of his cabin, he did not create a faint mental vision of her person for himself, but, more intimately affected, he scented distinctly the faint perfume she used, and could almost have sworn that he had been awakened by the soft rustle of her dress. He even sat up listening in the dark for a time, then sighed and lay down again, not agitated but, on the contrary, oppressed by the sensation of something that had happened to him and could not be undone.

CHAPTER III

In the afternoon he lounged into the editorial office, carrying with affected nonchalance that weight of the irremediable he had felt laid on him suddenly in the small hours of the night - that consciousness of something that could no longer be helped. His patronising friend informed him at once that he had made the acquaintance of the Moorsom party last night. At the Dunsters, of course. Dinner.

"Very quiet. Nobody there. It was much better for the business. I say . . ."

Renouard, his hand grasping the back of a chair, stared down at him dumbly.

"Phew! That's a stunning girl. . . Why do you want to sit on that chair? It's uncomfortable!"

"I wasn't going to sit on it." Renouard walked slowly to the window, glad to find in himself enough self-control to let go the chair instead of raising it on high and bringing it down on the Editor's head.

"Willie kept on gazing at her with tears in his boiled eyes. You should have seen him bending sentimentally over her at dinner."

"Don't," said Renouard in such an anguished tone that the Editor turned right round to look at his back.

"You push your dislike of young Dunster too far. It's positively morbid," he disapproved mildly. "We can't be all beautiful after thirty. . . . I talked a little, about you mostly, to the professor. He appeared to be interested in the silk plant - if only as a change from the great subject. Miss Moorsom didn't seem to mind when I confessed to her that I had taken you into the confidence of the thing. Our Willie approved too. Old Dunster with his white beard seemed to give me his blessing. All those people have a great opinion of you, simply because I told them that you've led every sort of life one can think of before you got struck on exploration. They want you to make suggestions. What do you think 'Master Arthur' is likely to have taken to?"

"Something easy," muttered Renouard without unclenching his teeth.

"Hunting man. Athlete. Don't be hard on the chap. He may be riding boundaries, or droving cattle, or humping his swag about the back-blocks away to the devil - somewhere. He may be even prospecting at the back of beyond - this very moment."

"Or lying dead drunk in a roadside pub. It's late enough in the day for that."

The Editor looked up instinctively. The clock was pointing at a quarter to five. "Yes, it is," he admitted. "But it needn't be. And he may have lit out into the Western Pacific all of a sudden - say in a trading schooner. Though I really don't see in what capacity. Still . . . "

"Or he may be passing at this very moment under this very window."

"Not he . . . and I wish you would get away from it to where one can see your face. I hate talking to a man's back. You stand there like a hermit on a sea-shore growling to yourself. I tell you what it is, Geoffrey, you don't like mankind."

"I don't make my living by talking about mankind's affairs," Renouard defended himself. But he came away obediently and sat down in the armchair. "How can you be so certain that your man isn't down there in the street?" he asked. "It's neither more nor less probable than every single one of your other suppositions."

Placated by Renouard's docility the Editor gazed at him for a while. "Aha! I'll tell you how. Learn then that we have begun the campaign. We have telegraphed his description to the police of every township up and down the land. And what's more we've ascertained definitely that he hasn't been in this town for the last three months at least. How much longer he's been away we can't tell."

"That's very curious."

"It's very simple. Miss Moorsom wrote to him, to the post office here directly she returned to London after her excursion into the country to see the old butler. Well - her letter is still lying there. It has not been called for. Ergo, this town is not his usual abode. Personally, I never thought it was. But he cannot fail to turn up some time or other. Our main hope lies just in the certitude that he must come to town sooner or later. Remember he doesn't know that the butler is dead, and he will want to inquire for a letter. Well, he'll find a note from Miss Moorsom."

Renouard, silent, thought that it was likely enough. His profound distaste for this conversation was betrayed by an air of weariness darkening his energetic sun-tanned features, and by the augmented dreaminess of his eyes. The Editor noted it as a further proof of that immoral detachment from mankind, of that callousness of sentiment fostered by the unhealthy conditions of solitude - according to his own favourite theory. Aloud he observed that as long as a man had not given up correspondence he could not be looked upon as lost. Fugitive criminals had been tracked in that way by justice, he reminded his friend; then suddenly changed the bearing of the subject somewhat by asking if Renouard had heard from his people lately, and if every member of his large tribe was well and happy.

"Yes, thanks."

The tone was curt, as if repelling a liberty. Renouard did not like being asked about his people, for whom he had a profound and remorseful affection. He had not seen a single human being to whom he was related, for many years, and he was extremely different from them all.

On the very morning of his arrival from his island he had gone to a set of pigeon-holes in Willie Dunster's outer office and had taken out from a compartment labelled "Malata" a very small accumulation of envelopes, a few addressed to himself, and one addressed to his assistant, all to the care of the firm, W. Dunster and Co. As opportunity offered, the firm used to send them on to Malata either by a man-of-war schooner going on a cruise, or by some trading craft proceeding that way. But for the last four months there had been no opportunity.

"You going to stay here some time?" asked the Editor, after a longish silence.

Renouard, perfunctorily, did see no reason why he should make a long stay.

"For health, for your mental health, my boy," rejoined the newspaper man. "To get used to human faces so that they don't hit you in the eye so hard when you walk about the streets. To get friendly with your kind. I suppose that assistant of yours can be trusted to look after things?"

"There's the half-caste too. The Portuguese. He knows what's to be done."

"Aha!" The Editor looked sharply at his friend. "What's his name?"

"Who's name?"

"The assistant's you picked up on the sly behind my back."

Renouard made a slight movement of impatience.

"I met him unexpectedly one evening. I thought he would do as well as another. He had come from up country and didn't seem happy in a town. He told me his name was Walter. I did not ask him for proofs, you know."

"I don't think you get on very well with him."

"Why? What makes you think so."

"I don't know. Something reluctant in your manner when he's in question."

"Really. My manner! I don't think he's a great subject for conversation, perhaps. Why not drop him?"

"Of course! You wouldn't confess to a mistake. Not you. Nevertheless I have my suspicions about it."

Renouard got up to go, but hesitated, looking down at the seated Editor.

"How funny," he said at last with the utmost seriousness, and was making for the door, when the voice of his friend stopped him.

"You know what has been said of you? That you couldn't get on with anybody you couldn't kick. Now, confess - is there any truth in the soft impeachment?"

"No," said Renouard. "Did you print that in your paper."

"No. I didn't quite believe it. But I will tell you what I believe. I believe that when your heart is set on some object you are a man that doesn't count the cost to yourself or others. And this shall get printed some day."

"Obituary notice?" Renouard dropped negligently.

"Certain - some day."

"Do you then regard yourself as immortal?"

"No, my boy. I am not immortal. But the voice of the press goes on for ever. . . . And it will say that this was the secret of your great success in a task where better men than you - meaning no offence - did fail repeatedly."

"Success," muttered Renouard, pulling-to the office door after him with considerable energy. And the letters of the word PRIVATE like a row of white eyes seemed to stare after his back sinking down the staircase of that temple of publicity.

Renouard had no doubt that all the means of publicity would be put at the service of love and used for the discovery of the loved man. He did not wish him dead. He did not wish him any harm. We are all equipped with a fund of humanity which is not exhausted without many and repeated provocations - and this man had done him no evil. But before Renouard had left old Dunster's house, at the conclusion of the call he made there that very afternoon, he had discovered in himself the desire that the search might last long. He never really flattered himself that it might fail. It seemed to him that there was no other course in this world for himself, for all mankind, but resignation. And he could not help thinking that Professor Moorsom had arrived at the same conclusion too.

Professor Moorsom, slight frame of middle height, a thoughtful keen head under the thick wavy hair, veiled dark eyes under straight eyebrows, and with an inward gaze which when disengaged and arriving at one seemed to issue from an obscure dream of books, from the limbo of meditation, showed himself extremely gracious to him. Renouard guessed in him a man whom an incurable habit of investigation and analysis had made gentle and indulgent; inapt for action, and more sensitive to the thoughts than to the events of existence. Withal not crushed, sub-ironic without a trace of acidity, and with a simple manner which put people at ease quickly. They had a long conversation on the terrace commanding an extended view of the town and the harbour.

The splendid immobility of the bay resting under his gaze, with its grey spurs and shining indentations, helped Renouard to regain his self-possession, which he had felt shaken, in coming out on the terrace, into the setting of the most powerful emotion of his life, when he had sat within a foot of Miss Moorsom with fire in his breast, a humming in his ears, and in a complete disorder of his mind. There was the very garden seat on which he had been enveloped in the radiant spell. And presently he was sitting on it again with the professor talking of her. Near by the patriarchal Dunster leaned forward in a wicker arm-chair, benign and a little deaf, his big hand to his ear with the innocent eagerness of his advanced age remembering the fires of life.

It was with a sort of apprehension that Renouard looked forward to seeing Miss Moorsom. And strangely enough it resembled the state of mind of a man who fears disenchantment more than sortilege. But he need not have been afraid. Directly he saw her in a distance at the other end of the terrace he shuddered to the roots of his hair. With her approach the power of speech left him for a time. Mrs. Dunster and her aunt were accompanying her. All these people sat down; it was an intimate circle into which Renouard felt himself cordially admitted; and the talk was of the great search which occupied all their minds. Discretion was expected by these people, but of reticence as to the object of the journey there could be no question. Nothing but ways and means and arrangements could be talked about.

By fixing his eyes obstinately on the ground, which gave him an air of reflective sadness, Renouard managed to recover his self-possession. He used it to keep his voice in a low key and to measure his words on the great subject. And he took care with a great inward effort to make them reasonable without giving them a discouraging complexion. For he did not want the quest to be given up, since it would mean her going away with her two attendant grey-heads to the other side of the world.

He was asked to come again, to come often and take part in the counsels of all these people captivated by the sentimental enterprise of a declared love. On taking Miss Moorsom's hand he looked up, would have liked to say something, but found himself voiceless, with his lips suddenly sealed. She returned the pressure of his fingers, and he left her with her eyes vaguely staring beyond him, an air of listening for an expected sound, and the faintest possible smile on her lips. A smile not for him, evidently, but the reflection of some deep and inscrutable thought.

CHAPTER IV

He went on board his schooner. She lay white, and as if suspended, in the crepuscular atmosphere of sunset mingling with the ashy gleam of the vast anchorage. He tried to keep his thoughts as sober, as reasonable, as measured as his words had been, lest they should get away from him and cause some sort of moral disaster. What he was afraid of in the coming night was sleeplessness and the endless strain of that wearisome task. It had to be faced however. He lay on his back, sighing profoundly in the dark, and suddenly beheld his very own self, carrying a small bizarre lamp, reflected in a long mirror inside a room in an empty and unfurnished palace. In this startling image of himself he recognised somebody he had to follow - the frightened guide of his dream. He traversed endless galleries, no end of lofty halls, innumerable doors. He lost himself utterly - he found his way again. Room succeeded room. At last the lamp went out, and he stumbled against some object which, when he stooped for it, he found to be very cold and heavy to lift. The sickly white light of dawn showed him the head of a statue. Its marble hair was done in the bold lines of a helmet, on its lips the chisel had left a faint smile, and it resembled Miss Moorsom. While he was staring at it fixedly, the head began to grow light in his fingers, to diminish and crumble to pieces, and at last turned into a handful of dust, which was blown away by a puff of

Joseph Conrad

wind so chilly that he woke up with a desperate shiver and leaped headlong out of his bed-place. The day had really come. He sat down by the cabin table, and taking his head between his hands, did not stir for a very long time.

Very quiet, he set himself to review this dream. The lamp, of course, he connected with the search for a man. But on closer examination he perceived that the reflection of himself in the mirror was not really the true Renouard, but somebody else whose face he could not remember. In the deserted palace he recognised a sinister adaptation by his brain of the long corridors with many doors, in the great building in which his friend's newspaper was lodged on the first floor. The marble head with Miss Moorsom's face! Well! What other face could he have dreamed of? And her complexion was fairer than Parian marble, than the heads of angels. The wind at the end was the morning breeze entering through the open porthole and touching his face before the schooner could swing to the chilly gust.

Yes! And all this rational explanation of the fantastic made it only more mysterious and weird. There was something daemonic in that dream. It was one of those experiences which throw a man out of conformity with the established order of his kind and make him a creature of obscure suggestions.

Henceforth, without ever trying to resist, he went every afternoon to the house where she lived. He went there as passively as if in a dream. He could never make out how he had attained the footing of intimacy in the Dunster mansion above the bay - whether on the ground of personal merit or as the pioneer of the vegetable silk industry. It must have been the last, because he remembered distinctly, as distinctly as in a dream, hearing old Dunster once telling him that his next public task would be a careful survey of the Northern Districts to discover tracts suitable for the cultivation of the silk plant. The old man wagged his beard at him sagely. It was indeed as absurd as a dream.

Willie of course would be there in the evening. But he was more of a figure out of a nightmare, hovering about the circle of chairs in his dress-clothes like a gigantic, repulsive, and sentimental bat. "Do away with the beastly cocoons all over the world," he buzzed in his blurred, water-logged voice. He affected a great horror of insects of all kinds. One evening he appeared with a red flower in his button-hole. Nothing could have been more disgustingly fantastic. And he would also say to Renouard: "You may yet change the history of our country. For economic conditions do shape the history of nations. Eh? What?" And he would turn to Miss Moorsom for approval, lowering protectingly his spatulous nose and looking up with feeling from under his absurd eyebrows, which grew thin, in the manner of canebrakes, out of his spongy skin. For this large, bilious creature was an economist and a sentimentalist, facile to tears, and a member of the Cobden Club.

In order to see as little of him as possible Renouard began coming earlier so as to get away before his arrival, without curtailing too much the hours of secret contemplation for which he lived. He had given up trying to deceive himself. His resignation was without bounds. He accepted the immense misfortune of being in love with a woman who was in search of another man only to throw herself into his arms. With such desperate precision he defined in his thoughts the situation, the consciousness of which traversed like a sharp arrow the sudden silences of general conversation. The only thought before which he quailed was the thought that this could not last; that it must come to an end. He feared it instinctively as a sick man may fear death. For it seemed to him that it must be the death of him followed by a lightless, bottomless pit. But his resignation was not spared the torments of jealousy: the cruel, insensate, poignant, and imbecile jealousy, when it seems that a woman betrays us simply by this that she exists, that she breathes - and when the deep movements of her nerves or her soul become a matter of distracting suspicion, of killing doubt, of mortal anxiety.

In the peculiar condition of their sojourn Miss Moorsom went out very little. She accepted this seclusion at the Dunsters' mansion as in a hermitage, and lived there, watched over by a group of old people, with the lofty endurance of a condescending and strong-headed goddess. It was impossible to say if she suffered from anything in the world, and whether this was the insensibility of a great passion concentrated on itself, or a perfect restraint of manner, or the indifference of superiority so complete as to be sufficient to itself. But it was visible to Renouard that she took some pleasure in talking to him at times. Was it because he was the only person near her age? Was this, then, the secret of his admission to the circle?

He admired her voice as well poised as her movements, as her attitudes. He himself had always been a man of tranquil tones. But the power of fascination had torn him out of his very nature so completely that to preserve his habitual calmness from going to pieces had become a terrible effort.

He used to go from her on board the schooner exhausted, broken, shaken up, as though he had been put to the most exquisite torture. When he saw her approaching he always had a moment of hallucination. She was a misty and fair creature, fitted for invisible music, for the shadows of love, for the murmurs of waters. After a time (he could not be always staring at the ground) he would summon up all his resolution and look at her. There was a sparkle in the clear obscurity of her eyes; and when she turned them on him they seemed to give a new meaning to life. He would say to himself that another man would have found long before the happy release of madness, his wits burnt to cinders in that radiance. But no such luck for him. His wits had come unscathed through the furnaces of hot suns, of blazing deserts, of flaming angers against the weaknesses of men and the obstinate cruelties of hostile nature.

Being sane he had to be constantly on his guard against falling into adoring silences or breaking out into wild speeches. He had to keep watch on his eyes, his limbs, on the muscles of his face. Their conversations were such as they could be between these two people: she a young lady fresh from the thick twilight of four million people and the artificiality of several London seasons; he the man of definite conquering tasks, the familiar of wide horizons, and in his very repose holding aloof from these agglomerations of units in which one loses one's importance even to oneself. They had no common conversational small change. They had to use the great pieces of general ideas, but they exchanged them trivially. It was no serious commerce. Perhaps she had not much of that coin. Nothing significant came from her. It could not be said that she had received from the contacts of the external world impressions of a personal kind, different from other women. What was ravishing in her was her quietness and, in her grave attitudes, the unfailing brilliance of her femininity. He did not know what there was under that ivory forehead so splendidly shaped, so gloriously crowned. He could not tell what were her thoughts, her feelings. Her replies were reflective, always preceded by a short silence, while he hung on her lips anxiously. He felt himself in the presence of a mysterious being in whom spoke an unknown voice, like the voice of oracles, bringing everlasting unrest to the heart.

He was thankful enough to sit in silence with secretly clenched teeth, devoured by jealousy - and nobody could have guessed that his quiet deferential bearing to all these grey-heads was the supreme effort of stoicism, that the man was engaged in keeping a sinister watch on his tortures lest his strength should fail him. As before, when grappling with other forces of nature, he could find in himself all sorts of courage except the courage to run away.

It was perhaps from the lack of subjects they could have in common that Miss Moorsom made him so often speak of his own life. He did not shrink from talking about himself, for he was free from that exacerbated, timid vanity which seals so many vain-glorious lips. He talked to her in his restrained voice, gazing at the tip of her shoe, and thinking that the time was bound to come soon when her very inattention would get weary of him. And indeed on stealing a glance he would see her dazzling and perfect, her eyes vague, staring in mournful immobility, with a drooping head that made him think of a tragic Venus arising before him, not from the foam of the sea, but from a distant, still more formless, mysterious, and potent immensity of mankind.

Joseph Conrad

CHAPTER V

One afternoon Renouard stepping out on the terrace found nobody there. It was for him, at the same time, a melancholy disappointment and a poignant relief.

The heat was great, the air was still, all the long windows of the house stood wide open. At the further end, grouped round a lady's work-table, several chairs disposed sociably suggested invisible occupants, a company of conversing shades. Renouard looked towards them with a sort of dread. A most elusive, faint sound of ghostly talk issuing from one of the rooms added to the illusion and stopped his already hesitating footsteps. He leaned over the balustrade of stone near a squat vase holding a tropical plant of a bizarre shape. Professor Moorsom coming up from the garden with a book under his arm and a white parasol held over his bare head, found him there and, closing the parasol, leaned over by his side with a remark on the increasing heat of the season. Renouard assented and changed his position a little; the other, after a short silence, administered unexpectedly a question which, like the blow of a club on the head, deprived Renouard of the power of speech and even thought, but, more cruel, left him quivering with apprehension, not of death but of everlasting torment. Yet the words were extremely simple.

"Something will have to be done soon. We can't remain in a state of suspended expectation for ever. Tell me what do you think of our chances?"

Renouard, speechless, produced a faint smile. The professor confessed in a jocular tone his impatience to complete the circuit of the globe and be done with it. It was impossible to remain quartered on the dear excellent Dunsters for an indefinite time. And then there were the lectures he had arranged to deliver in Paris. A serious matter.

That lectures by Professor Moorsom were a European event and that brilliant audiences would gather to hear them Renouard did not know. All he was aware of was the shock of this hint of departure. The menace of separation fell on his head like a thunderbolt. And he saw the absurdity of his emotion, for hadn't he lived all these days under the very cloud? The professor, his elbows spread out, looked down into the garden and went on unburdening his mind. Yes. The department of sentiment was directed by his daughter, and she had plenty of volunteered moral support; but he had to look after the practical side of life without assistance.

"I have the less hesitation in speaking to you about my anxiety, because I feel you are friendly to us and at the same time you are detached from all these sublimities - confound them."

"What do you mean?" murmured Renouard.

"I mean that you are capable of calm judgment. Here the atmosphere is simply detestable. Everybody has knuckled under to sentiment. Perhaps your deliberate opinion could influence . . ."

"You want Miss Moorsom to give it up?" The professor turned to the young man dismally.

"Heaven only knows what I want."

Renouard leaning his back against the balustrade folded his arms on his breast, appeared to meditate profoundly. His face, shaded softly by the broad brim of a planter's Panama hat, with the straight line of the nose level with the forehead, the eyes lost in the depth of the setting, and the chin well forward, had such a profile as may be seen amongst the bronzes of classical museums, pure under a crested helmet - recalled vaguely a Minerva's head.

"This is the most troublesome time I ever had in my life," exclaimed the professor testily.

"Surely the man must be worth it," muttered Renouard with a pang of jealousy traversing his breast like a self-inflicted stab.

Whether enervated by the heat or giving way to pent up irritation the professor surrendered himself to the mood of sincerity.

"He began by being a pleasantly dull boy. He developed into a pointlessly clever young man, without, I suspect, ever trying to understand anything. My daughter knew him from childhood. I am a busy man, and I confess that their engagement was a complete surprise to me. I wish their reasons for that step had been more naive. But simplicity was out of fashion in their set. From a worldly point of view he seems to have been a mere baby. Of course, now, I am assured that he is the victim of his noble confidence in the rectitude of his kind. But that's mere idealising of a sad reality. For my part I will tell you that from the very beginning I had the gravest doubts of his dishonesty. Unfortunately my clever daughter hadn't. And now we behold the reaction. No. To be earnestly dishonest one must be really poor. This was only a manifestation of his extremely refined cleverness. The complicated simpleton. He had an awful awakening though."

In such words did Professor Moorsom give his "young friend" to understand the state of his feelings toward the lost man. It was evident that the father of Miss Moorsom wished him to remain lost. Perhaps the unprecedented heat of the season made him long for the cool spaces of the Pacific, the sweep of the ocean's free wind along the promenade decks, cumbered with long chairs, of a ship steaming towards the Californian coast. To Renouard the philosopher appeared simply the most treacherous of fathers. He was amazed. But he was not at the end of his discoveries.

"He may be dead," the professor murmured.

"Why? People don't die here sooner than in Europe. If he had gone to hide in Italy, for instance, you wouldn't think of saying that."

"Well! And suppose he has become morally disintegrated. You know he was not a strong personality," the professor suggested moodily. "My daughter's future is in question here."

Renouard thought that the love of such a woman was enough to pull any broken man together - to drag a man out of his grave. And he thought this with inward despair, which kept him silent as much almost as his astonishment. At last he managed to stammer out a generous -

"Oh! Don't let us even suppose. . ."

The professor struck in with a sadder accent than before -

"It's good to be young. And then you have been a man of action, and necessarily a believer in success. But I have been looking too long at life not to distrust its surprises. Age! Age! Here I stand before you a man full of doubts and hesitation - spe lentus, timidus futuri."

He made a sign to Renouard not to interrupt, and in a lowered voice, as if afraid of being overheard, even there, in the solitude of the terrace -

"And the worst is that I am not even sure how far this sentimental pilgrimage is genuine. Yes. I doubt my own child. It's true that she's a woman. . . . "

Renouard detected with horror a tone of resentment, as if the professor had never forgiven his daughter for not dying instead of his son. The latter noticed the young man's stony stare.

"Ah! you don't understand. Yes, she's clever, open-minded, popular, and - well, charming. But you don't know what it is to have moved, breathed, existed, and even triumphed in the mere smother and froth of life - the brilliant froth. There thoughts, sentiments, opinions, feelings, actions too, are nothing but agitation in empty space - to amuse life - a sort of superior debauchery, exciting and fatiguing, meaning nothing, leading nowhere. She is the creature of that circle. And I ask myself if she is obeying the uneasiness of an instinct seeking its satisfaction, or is it a revulsion of feeling, or is she merely deceiving her own heart by this dangerous trifling with romantic images. And everything is possible - except sincerity, such as only stark, struggling humanity can know. No woman can stand that mode of life in which women rule, and remain a perfectly genuine, simple human being. Ah! There's some people coming out."

He moved off a pace, then turning his head: "Upon my word! I would be infinitely obliged to you if you could throw a little cold water. . . " and at a vaguely dismayed gesture of Renouard, he added: "Don't be afraid. You wouldn't be putting out a sacred fire."

Renouard could hardly find words for a protest: "I assure you that I never talk with Miss Moorsom - on - on - that. And if you, her father . . . "

"I envy you your innocence," sighed the professor. "A father is only an everyday person. Flat. Stale. Moreover, my child would naturally mistrust me. We belong to the same set. Whereas you carry with you the prestige of the unknown. You have proved yourself to be a force."

Thereupon the professor followed by Renouard joined the circle of all the inmates of the house assembled at the other end of the terrace about a tea-table; three white heads and that resplendent vision of woman's glory, the sight of which had the power to flutter his heart like a reminder of the mortality of his frame.

He avoided the seat by the side of Miss Moorsom. The others were talking together languidly. Unnoticed he looked at that woman so marvellous that centuries seemed to lie between them. He was oppressed and overcome at the thought of what she could give to some man who really would be a force! What a glorious struggle with this amazon. What noble burden for the victorious strength.

Dear old Mrs. Dunster was dispensing tea, looking from time to time with interest towards Miss Moorsom. The aged statesman having eaten a raw tomato and drunk a glass of milk (a habit of his early farming days, long before politics, when, pioneer of wheat-growing, he demonstrated the possibility of raising crops on ground looking barren enough to discourage a magician), smoothed his white beard, and struck lightly Renouard's knee with his big wrinkled hand.

"You had better come back to-night and dine with us quietly."

He liked this young man, a pioneer, too, in more than one direction. Mrs. Dunster added: "Do. It will be very quiet. I don't even know if Willie will be home for dinner." Renouard murmured his thanks, and left the terrace to go on board the schooner. While lingering in the drawing-room doorway he heard the resonant voice of old Dunster uttering oracularly -

". . . the leading man here some day. . . . Like me."

Renouard let the thin summer portiere of the doorway fall behind him. The voice of Professor Moorsom said -

"I am told that he has made an enemy of almost every man who had to work with him."

"That's nothing. He did his work. . . . Like me."

"He never counted the cost they say. Not even of lives."

Renouard understood that they were talking of him. Before he could move away, Mrs. Dunster struck in placidly -

"Don't let yourself be shocked by the tales you may hear of him, my dear. Most of it is envy."

Then he heard Miss Moorsom's voice replying to the old lady -

"Oh! I am not easily deceived. I think I may say I have an instinct for truth."

He hastened away from that house with his heart full of dread.

CHAPTER VI

On board the schooner, lying on the settee on his back with the knuckles of his hands pressed over his eyes, he made up his mind that he would not return to that house for dinner - that he would never go back there any more. He made up his mind some twenty times. The knowledge that he had only to go up on the quarter deck, utter quietly the words: "Man the windlass," and that the schooner springing into life would run a hundred miles out to sea before sunrise, deceived his struggling will. Nothing easier! Yet, in the end, this young man, almost ill-famed for his ruthless daring, the inflexible leader of two tragically successful expeditions, shrank from that act of savage energy, and began, instead, to hunt for excuses.

No! It was not for him to run away like an incurable who cuts his throat. He finished dressing and looked at his own impassive face in the saloon mirror scornfully. While being pulled on shore in the gig, he remembered suddenly the wild beauty of a waterfall seen when hardly more than a boy, years ago, in Menado. There was a legend of a governor-general of the Dutch East Indies, on official tour, committing suicide on that spot by leaping into the chasm. It was supposed that a painful disease had made him weary of life. But was there ever a visitation like his own, at the same time binding one to life and so cruelly mortal!

The dinner was indeed quiet. Willie, given half an hour's grace, failed to turn up, and his chair remained vacant by the side of Miss Moorsom. Renouard had the professor's sister on his left, dressed in an expensive gown becoming her age. That maiden lady in her wonderful preservation reminded Renouard somehow of a wax flower under glass. There were no traces of the dust of life's battles on her anywhere. She did not like him very much in the afternoons, in his white drill suit and planter's hat, which seemed to her an unduly Bohemian costume for calling in a house where there were ladies. But in the evening, lithe and elegant in his dress clothes and with his pleasant, slightly veiled voice, he always made her conquest afresh. He might have been anybody distinguished - the son of a duke. Falling under that charm probably (and also because her brother had given her a hint), she attempted to open her heart to Renouard, who was watching with all the power of his soul her niece across the table. She spoke to him as frankly as though that miserable mortal envelope, emptied of everything but hopeless passion, were indeed the son of a duke.

Inattentive, he heard her only in snatches, till the final confidential burst: ". . . glad if you would express an opinion. Look at her, so charming, such a great favourite, so generally admired! It would be too sad. We all hoped she would make a brilliant marriage with somebody very rich and of high position, have a house in London and in the country, and entertain us all splendidly. She's so eminently fitted for it. She has such hosts of distinguished friends! And then - this instead! . . . My heart really aches."

Her well-bred if anxious whisper was covered by the voice of professor Moorsom discoursing subtly down

the short length of the dinner table on the Imper-
manency of the Measurable to his venerable disciple. It
might have been a chapter in a new and popular book
of Moorsonian philosophy. Patriarchal and delighted,
old Dunster leaned forward a little, his eyes shining
youthfully, two spots of colour at the roots of his white
beard; and Renouard, glancing at the senile excitement,
recalled the words heard on those subtle lips, adopted
their scorn for his own, saw their truth before this man
ready to be amused by the side of the grave. Yes!
Intellectual debauchery in the froth of existence! Froth
and fraud!

On the same side of the table Miss Moorsom never
once looked towards her father, all her grace as if
frozen, her red lips compressed, the faintest rosiness
under her dazzling complexion, her black eyes burning
motionless, and the very coppery gleams of light lying
still on the waves and undulation of her hair. Renouard
fancied himself overturning the table, smashing crystal
and china, treading fruit and flowers under foot,
seizing her in his arms, carrying her off in a tumult of
shrieks from all these people, a silent frightened
mortal, into some profound retreat as in the age of
Cavern men. Suddenly everybody got up, and he
hastened to rise too, finding himself out of breath and
quite unsteady on his feet.

On the terrace the philosopher, after lighting a cigar,
slipped his hand condescendingly under his "dear
young friend's" arm. Renouard regarded him now with
the profoundest mistrust. But the great man seemed
really to have a liking for his young friend - one of
those mysterious sympathies, disregarding the
differences of age and position, which in this case
might have been explained by the failure of philosophy

to meet a very real worry of a practical kind.

After a turn or two and some casual talk the professor said suddenly: "My late son was in your school - do you know? I can imagine that had he lived and you had ever met you would have understood each other. He too was inclined to action."

He sighed, then, shaking off the mournful thought and with a nod at the dusky part of the terrace where the dress of his daughter made a luminous stain: "I really wish you would drop in that quarter a few sensible, discouraging words."

Renouard disengaged himself from that most perfidious of men under the pretence of astonishment, and stepping back a pace -

"Surely you are making fun of me, Professor Moorsom," he said with a low laugh, which was really a sound of rage.

"My dear young friend! It's no subject for jokes, to me. You don't seem to have any notion of your prestige," he added, walking away towards the chairs.

"Humbug!" thought Renouard, standing still and looking after him. "And yet! And yet! What if it were true?"

He advanced then towards Miss Moorsom. Posed on the seat on which they had first spoken to each other, it was her turn to watch him coming on. But many of the windows were not lighted that evening. It was dark over there. She appeared to him luminous in her clear dress, a figure without shape, a face without features, awaiting his approach, till he got quite near to her, sat down, and they had exchanged a few insignificant words. Gradually she came out like a magic painting of charm, fascination, and desire, glowing mysteriously on the dark background. Something imperceptible in the lines of her attitude, in the modulations of her voice, seemed to soften that suggestion of calm unconscious pride which enveloped her always like a mantle. He, sensitive like a bond slave to the moods of the master, was moved by the subtle relenting of her grace to an infinite tenderness. He fought down the impulse to seize her by the hand, lead her down into the garden away under the big trees, and throw himself at her feet uttering words of love. His emotion was so strong that he had to cough slightly, and not knowing what to talk to her about he began to tell her of his mother and sisters. All the family were coming to London to live there, for some little time at least.

"I hope you will go and tell them something of me. Something seen," he said pressingly.

By this miserable subterfuge, like a man about to part with his life, he hoped to make her remember him a little longer.

"Certainly," she said. "I'll be glad to call when I get back. But that 'when' may be a long time."

He heard a light sigh. A cruel jealous curiosity made him ask -

"Are you growing weary, Miss Moorsom?"

A silence fell on his low spoken question.

"Do you mean heart-weary?" sounded Miss Moorsom's voice. "You don't know me, I see."

"Ah! Never despair," he muttered.

"This, Mr. Renouard, is a work of reparation. I stand for truth here. I can't think of myself."

He could have taken her by the throat for every word seemed an insult to his passion; but he only said -

"I never doubted the - the - nobility of your purpose."

"And to hear the word weariness pronounced in this connection surprises me. And from a man too who, I understand, has never counted the cost."

"You are pleased to tease me," he said, directly he had recovered his voice and had mastered his anger. It was as if Professor Moorsom had dropped poison in his ear which was spreading now and tainting his passion, his very jealousy. He mistrusted every word that came from those lips on which his life hung. "How can you know anything of men who do not count the cost?" he asked in his gentlest tones.

"From hearsay - a little."

"Well, I assure you they are like the others, subject to suffering, victims of spells. . . ."

"One of them, at least, speaks very strangely."

She dismissed the subject after a short silence. "Mr. Renouard, I had a disappointment this morning. This mail brought me a letter from the widow of the old butler - you know. I expected to learn that she had heard from - from here. But no. No letter arrived home since we left."

Her voice was calm. His jealousy couldn't stand much more of this sort of talk; but he was glad that nothing had turned up to help the search; glad blindly, unreasonably - only because it would keep her longer in his sight - since she wouldn't give up.

"I am too near her," he thought, moving a little further on the seat. He was afraid in the revulsion of feeling of flinging himself on her hands, which were lying on her lap, and covering them with kisses. He was afraid. Nothing, nothing could shake that spell - not if she were ever so false, stupid, or degraded. She was fate itself. The extent of his misfortune plunged him in such a stupor that he failed at first to hear the sound of voices and footsteps inside the drawing-room. Willie had come home - and the Editor was with him.

They burst out on the terrace babbling noisily, and then pulling themselves together stood still, surprising - and as if themselves surprised.

CHAPTER VII

They had been feasting a poet from the bush, the latest discovery of the Editor. Such discoveries were the business, the vocation, the pride and delight of the only apostle of letters in the hemisphere, the solitary patron of culture, the Slave of the Lamp - as he subscribed himself at the bottom of the weekly literary page of his paper. He had had no difficulty in persuading the virtuous Willie (who had festive instincts) to help in the good work, and now they had left the poet lying asleep on the hearthrug of the editorial room and had rushed to the Dunster mansion wildly. The Editor had another discovery to announce. Swaying a little where he stood he opened his mouth very wide to shout the one word "Found!" Behind him Willie flung both his hands above his head and let them fall dramatically. Renouard saw the four white-headed people at the end of the terrace rise all together from their chairs with an effect of sudden panic.

"I tell you - he - is - found," the patron of letters shouted emphatically.

"What is this!" exclaimed Renouard in a choked voice. Miss Moorsom seized his wrist suddenly, and at that contact fire ran through all his veins, a hot stillness descended upon him in which he heard the blood - or the fire - beating in his ears. He made a movement as if to rise, but was restrained by the convulsive pressure on his wrist.

"No, no." Miss Moorsom's eyes stared black as night, searching the space before her. Far away the Editor strutted forward, Willie following with his ostentatious manner of carrying his bulky and oppressive carcass which, however, did not remain exactly perpendicular for two seconds together.

"The innocent Arthur . . . Yes. We've got him," the Editor became very business-like. "Yes, this letter has done it."

He plunged into an inside pocket for it, slapped the scrap of paper with his open palm. "From that old woman. William had it in his pocket since this morning when Miss Moorsom gave it to him to show me. Forgot all about it till an hour ago. Thought it was of no importance. Well, no! Not till it was properly read."

Renouard and Miss Moorsom emerged from the shadows side by side, a well-matched couple, animated yet statuesque in their calmness and in their pallor. She had let go his wrist. On catching sight of Renouard the Editor exclaimed:

"What - you here!" in a quite shrill voice.

There came a dead pause. All the faces had in them something dismayed and cruel.

"He's the very man we want," continued the Editor. "Excuse my excitement. You are the very man, Renouard. Didn't you tell me that your assistant called himself Walter? Yes? Thought so. But here's that old woman - the butler's wife - listen to this. She writes: All I can tell you, Miss, is that my poor husband directed his letters to the name of H. Walter."

Renouard's violent but repressed exclamation was lost in a general murmur and shuffle of feet. The Editor made a step forward, bowed with creditable steadiness.

"Miss Moorsom, allow me to congratulate you from the bottom of my heart on the happy - er - issue. . . "

"Wait," muttered Renouard irresolutely.

The Editor jumped on him in the manner of their old friendship. "Ah, you! You are a fine fellow too. With your solitary ways of life you will end by having no more discrimination than a savage. Fancy living with a gentleman for months and never guessing. A man, I am certain, accomplished, remarkable, out of the common, since he had been distinguished" (he bowed again) "by Miss Moorsom, whom we all admire."

She turned her back on him.

"I hope to goodness you haven't been leading him a dog's life, Geoffrey," the Editor addressed his friend in a whispered aside.

Renouard seized a chair violently, sat down, and propping his elbow on his knee leaned his head on his hand. Behind him the sister of the professor looked up to heaven and wrung her hands stealthily. Mrs. Dunster's hands were clasped forcibly under her chin, but she, dear soul, was looking sorrowfully at Willie. The model nephew! In this strange state! So very much flushed! The careful disposition of the thin hairs across Willie's bald spot was deplorably disarranged, and the spot itself was red and, as it were, steaming.

"What's the matter, Geoffrey?" The Editor seemed disconcerted by the silent attitudes round him, as though he had expected all these people to shout and dance. "You have him on the island - haven't you?"

"Oh, yes: I have him there," said Renouard, without looking up.

"Well, then!" The Editor looked helplessly around as if begging for response of some sort. But the only response that came was very unexpected. Annoyed at being left in the background, and also because very little drink made him nasty, the emotional Willie turned malignant all at once, and in a bibulous tone surprising in a man able to keep his balance so well -

"Aha! But you haven't got him here - not yet!" he sneered. "No! You haven't got him yet."

This outrageous exhibition was to the Editor like the lash to a jaded horse. He positively jumped.

"What of that? What do you mean? We - haven't - got - him - here. Of course he isn't here! But Geoffrey's schooner is here. She can be sent at once to fetch him here. No! Stay! There's a better plan. Why shouldn't you all sail over to Malata, professor? Save time! I am sure Miss Moorsom would prefer. . ."

With a gallant flourish of his arm he looked for Miss Moorsom. She had disappeared. He was taken aback somewhat.

"Ah! H'm. Yes. . . . Why not. A pleasure cruise, delightful ship, delightful season, delightful errand, del No! There are no objections. Geoffrey, I understand, has indulged in a bungalow three sizes too large for him. He can put you all up. It will be a pleasure for him. It will be the greatest privilege. Any man would be proud of being an agent of this happy reunion. I am proud of the little part I've played. He will consider it the greatest honour. Geoff, my boy, you had better be stirring to-morrow bright and early about the preparations for the trip. It would be criminal to lose a single day."

He was as flushed as Willie, the excitement keeping up the effect of the festive dinner. For a time Renouard, silent, as if he had not heard a word of all that babble, did not stir. But when he got up it was to advance towards the Editor and give him such a hearty slap on the back that the plump little man reeled in his tracks and looked quite frightened for a moment.

"You are a heaven-born discoverer and a first-rate manager. . .He's right. It's the only way. You can't resist the claim of sentiment, and you must even risk the voyage to Malata. . . " Renouard's voice sank. "A lonely spot," he added, and fell into thought under all these eyes converging on him in the sudden silence. His slow glance passed over all the faces in succession, remaining arrested on Professor Moorsom, stony eyed, a smouldering cigar in his fingers, and with his sister standing by his side.

"I shall be infinitely gratified if you consent to come. But, of course, you will. We shall sail to-morrow evening then. And now let me leave you to your happiness."

He bowed, very grave, pointed suddenly his finger at Willie who was swaying about with a sleepy frown. "Look at him. He's overcome with happiness. You had better put him to bed . . . " and disappeared while every head on the terrace was turned to Willie with varied expressions.

Renouard ran through the house. Avoiding the carriage road he fled down the steep short cut to the shore, where his gig was waiting. At his loud shout the sleeping Kanakas jumped up. He leaped in. "Shove off. Give way!" and the gig darted through the water. "Give way! Give way!" She flew past the wool-clippers sleeping at their anchors each with the open unwinking eye of the lamp in the rigging; she flew past the flagship of the Pacific squadron, a great mass all dark and silent, heavy with the slumbers of five hundred men, and where the invisible sentries heard his urgent "Give way! Give way!" in the night. The Kanakas, panting, rose off the thwarts at every stroke. Nothing could be fast enough for him! And he ran up the side of his schooner shaking the ladder noisily with his rush.

On deck he stumbled and stood still.

Wherefore this haste? To what end, since he knew well before he started that he had a pursuer from whom there was no escape.

As his foot touched the deck his will, his purpose he had been hurrying to save, died out within. It had been nothing less than getting the schooner under-way, letting her vanish silently in the night from amongst these sleeping ships. And now he was certain he could not do it. It was impossible! And he reflected that whether he lived or died such an act would lay him under a dark suspicion from which he shrank. No, there was nothing to be done.

He went down into the cabin and, before even unbuttoning his overcoat, took out of the drawer the letter addressed to his assistant; that letter which he had found in the pigeon-hole labelled "Malata" in young Dunster's outer office, where it had been waiting for three months some occasion for being forwarded. From the moment of dropping it in the drawer he had utterly forgotten its existence - till now, when the man's name had come out so clamorously. He glanced at the common envelope, noted the shaky and laborious handwriting: H. Walter, Esqre. Undoubtedly the very last letter the old butler had posted before his illness, and in answer clearly to one from "Master Arthur" instructing him to address in the future: "Care of Messrs. W. Dunster and Co." Renouard made as if to open the envelope, but paused, and, instead, tore the letter deliberately in two, in four, in eight. With his hand full of pieces of paper he returned on deck and scattered them overboard on the dark water, in which they vanished instantly.

He did it slowly, without hesitation or remorse. H. Walter, Esqre, in Malata. The innocent Arthur - What was his name? The man sought for by that woman who as she went by seemed to draw all the passion of the earth to her, without effort, not deigning to notice, naturally, as other women breathed the air. But Renouard was no longer jealous of her very existence. Whatever its meaning it was not for that man he had picked up casually on obscure impulse, to get rid of the tiresome expostulations of a so-called friend; a man of whom he really knew nothing - and now a dead man.

In Malata. Oh, yes! He was there secure enough, untroubled in his grave. In Malata. To bury him was the last service Renouard had rendered to his assistant before leaving the island on this trip to town.

Like many men ready enough for arduous enterprises Renouard was inclined to evade the small complications of existence. This trait of his character was composed of a little indolence, some disdain, and a shrinking from contests with certain forms of vulgarity - like a man who would face a lion and go out of his way to avoid a toad. His intercourse with the meddlesome journalist was that merely outward intimacy without sympathy some young men get drawn into easily. It had amused him rather to keep that "friend" in the dark about the fate of his assistant. Renouard had never needed other company than his own, for there was in him something of the sensitiveness of a dreamer who is easily jarred. He had said to himself that the all-knowing one would only preach again about the evils of solitude and worry his head off in favour of some forlornly useless protege of his. Also the inquisitiveness of the Editor had irritated him and had closed his lips in sheer disgust.

And now he contemplated the noose of consequences drawing tight around him.

It was the memory of that diplomatic reticence which on the terrace had stiffled his first cry which would have told them all that the man sought for was not to be met on earth any more. He shrank from the absurdity of hearing the all-knowing one, and not very sober at that, turning on him with righteous reproaches -

"You never told me. You gave me to understand that your assistant was alive, and now you say he's dead. Which is it? Were you lying then or are you lying now?" No! the thought of such a scene was not to be borne. He had sat down appalled, thinking: "What shall I do now?"

His courage had oozed out of him. Speaking the truth meant the Moorsoms going away at once - while it seemed to him that he would give the last shred of his rectitude to secure a day more of her company. He sat on - silent. Slowly, from confused sensations, from his talk with the professor, the manner of the girl herself, the intoxicating familiarity of her sudden hand-clasp, there had come to him a half glimmer of hope. The other man was dead. Then! . . . Madness, of course - but he could not give it up. He had listened to that confounded busybody arranging everything - while all these people stood around assenting, under the spell of that dead romance. He had listened scornful and silent. The glimmers of hope, of opportunity, passed before his eyes. He had only to sit still and say nothing. That and no more. And what was truth to him in the face of that great passion which had flung him prostrate in spirit at her adored feet!

And now it was done! Fatality had willed it! With the eyes of a mortal struck by the maddening thunderbolt of the gods, Renouard looked up to the sky, an immense black pall dusted over with gold, on which great shudders seemed to pass from the breath of life affirming its sway.

CHAPTER VIII

At last, one morning, in a clear spot of a glassy horizon charged with heraldic masses of black vapours, the island grew out from the sea, showing here and there its naked members of basaltic rock through the rents of heavy foliage. Later, in the great spilling of all the riches of sunset, Malata stood out green and rosy before turning into a violet shadow in the autumnal light of the expiring day. Then came the night. In the faint airs the schooner crept on past a sturdy squat headland, and it was pitch dark when her headsails ran down, she turned short on her heel, and her anchor bit into the sandy bottom on the edge of the outer reef; for it was too dangerous then to attempt entering the little bay full of shoals. After the last solemn flutter of the mainsail the murmuring voices of the Moorsom party lingered, very frail, in the black stillness.

They were sitting aft, on chairs, and nobody made a move. Early in the day, when it had become evident that the wind was failing, Renouard, basing his advice on the shortcomings of his bachelor establishment, had urged on the ladies the advisability of not going ashore in the middle of the night. Now he approached them in a constrained manner (it was astonishing the constraint that had reigned between him and his guests all through the passage) and renewed his arguments. No one ashore would dream of his bringing any visitors with him. Nobody would even think of coming off. There was only one old canoe on the plantation. And landing in the schooner's boats would be awkward in the dark. There was the risk of getting aground on some shallow patches. It would be best to spend the rest of the night on board.

There was really no opposition. The professor smoking a pipe, and very comfortable in an ulster buttoned over his tropical clothes, was the first to speak from his long chair.

"Most excellent advice."

Next to him Miss Moorsom assented by a long silence. Then in a voice as of one coming out of a dream -

"And so this is Malata," she said. "I have often wondered . . ."

A shiver passed through Renouard. She had wondered! What about? Malata was himself. He and Malata were one. And she had wondered! She had . . .

The professor's sister leaned over towards Renouard. Through all these days at sea the man's - the found man's - existence had not been alluded to on board the schooner. That reticence was part of the general constraint lying upon them all. She, herself, certainly had not been exactly elated by this finding - poor Arthur, without money, without prospects. But she felt moved by the sentiment and romance of the situation.

"Isn't it wonderful," she whispered out of her white wrap, "to think of poor Arthur sleeping there, so near to our dear lovely Felicia , and not knowing the immense joy in store for him to-morrow."

There was such artificiality in the wax-flower lady that nothing in this speech touched Renouard. It was but the simple anxiety of his heart that he was voicing when he muttered gloomily -

"No one in the world knows what to-morrow may hold in store."

The mature lady had a recoil as though he had said something impolite. What a harsh thing to say - instead of finding something nice and appropriate. On board, where she never saw him in evening clothes, Renouard's resemblance to a duke's son was not so apparent to her. Nothing but his - ah - bohemianism remained. She rose with a sort of ostentation.

"It's late - and since we are going to sleep on board to-night . . ." she said. "But it does seem so cruel."

The professor started up eagerly, knocking the ashes out of his pipe. "Infinitely more sensible, my dear Emma."

Renouard waited behind Miss Moorsom's chair.

She got up slowly, moved one step forward, and paused looking at the shore. The blackness of the island blotted out the stars with its vague mass like a low thundercloud brooding over the waters and ready to burst into flame and crashes.

"And so - this is Malata," she repeated dreamily, moving towards the cabin door. The clear cloak hanging from her shoulders, the ivory face - for the night had put out nothing of her but the gleams of her hair - made her resemble a shining dream-woman uttering words of wistful inquiry. She disappeared without a sign, leaving Renouard penetrated to the very marrow by the sounds that came from her body like a mysterious resonance of an exquisite instrument.

He stood stock still. What was this accidental touch which had evoked the strange accent of her voice? He dared not answer that question. But he had to answer the question of what was to be done now. Had the moment of confession come? The thought was enough to make one's blood run cold.

It was as if those people had a premonition of something. In the taciturn days of the passage he had noticed their reserve even amongst themselves. The professor smoked his pipe moodily in retired spots. Renouard had caught Miss Moorsom's eyes resting on himself more than once, with a peculiar and grave expression. He fancied that she avoided all opportunities of conversation. The maiden lady seemed to nurse a grievance. And now what had he to do?

The lights on the deck had gone out one after the other. The schooner slept.

About an hour after Miss Moorsom had gone below without a sign or a word for him, Renouard got out of his hammock slung in the waist under the midship awning - for he had given up all the accommodation below to his guests. He got out with a sudden swift movement, flung off his sleeping jacket, rolled his pyjamas up his thighs, and stole forward, unseen by the one Kanaka of the anchor-watch. His white torso, naked like a stripped athlete's, glimmered, ghostly, in the deep shadows of the deck. Unnoticed he got out of the ship over the knight-heads, ran along the back rope, and seizing the dolphin-striker firmly with both hands, lowered himself into the sea without a splash.

He swam away, noiseless like a fish, and then struck boldly for the land, sustained, embraced, by the tepid water. The gentle, voluptuous heave of its breast swung him up and down slightly; sometimes a wavelet murmured in his ears; from time to time, lowering his feet, he felt for the bottom on a shallow patch to rest and correct his direction. He landed at the lower end of the bungalow garden, into the dead stillness of the island. There were no lights. The plantation seemed to sleep, as profoundly as the schooner. On the path a small shell cracked under his naked heel.

The faithful half-caste foreman going his rounds cocked his ears at the sharp sound. He gave one enormous start of fear at the sight of the swift white figure flying at him out of the night. He crouched in terror, and then sprang up and clicked his tongue in amazed recognition.

"Tse! Tse! The master!"

"Be quiet, Luiz, and listen to what I say."

Yes, it was the master, the strong master who was never known to raise his voice, the man blindly obeyed and never questioned. He talked low and rapidly in the quiet night, as if every minute were precious. On learning that three guests were coming to stay Luiz clicked his tongue rapidly. These clicks were the uniform, stenographic symbols of his emotions, and he could give them an infinite variety of meaning. He listened to the rest in a deep silence hardly affected by the low, "Yes, master," whenever Renouard paused.

"You understand?" the latter insisted. "No preparations are to be made till we land in the morning. And you are to say that Mr. Walter has gone off in a trading schooner on a round of the islands."

"Yes, master."

"No mistakes - mind!"

"No, master."

Renouard walked back towards the sea. Luiz, following him, proposed to call out half a dozen boys and man the canoe.

"Imbecile!"

"Tse! Tse! Tse!"

"Don't you understand that you haven't seen me?"

"Yes, master. But what a long swim. Suppose you drown."

"Then you can say of me and of Mr. Walter what you like. The dead don't mind."

Renouard entered the sea and heard a faint "Tse! Tse! Tse!" of concern from the half-caste, who had already lost sight of the master's dark head on the overshadowed water.

Renouard set his direction by a big star that, dipping on

the horizon, seemed to look curiously into his face. On this swim back he felt the mournful fatigue of all that length of the traversed road, which brought him no nearer to his desire. It was as if his love had sapped the invisible supports of his strength. There came a moment when it seemed to him that he must have swum beyond the confines of life. He had a sensation of eternity close at hand, demanding no effort - offering its peace. It was easy to swim like this beyond the confines of life looking at a star. But the thought: "They will think I dared not face them and committed suicide," caused a revolt of his mind which carried him on. He returned on board, as he had left, unheard and unseen. He lay in his hammock utterly exhausted and with a confused feeling that he had been beyond the confines of life, somewhere near a star, and that it was very quiet there.

CHAPTER IX

Sheltered by the squat headland from the first morning sparkle of the sea the little bay breathed a delicious freshness. The party from the schooner landed at the bottom of the garden. They exchanged insignificant words in studiously casual tones. The professor's sister put up a long-handled eye-glass as if to scan the novel surroundings, but in reality searching for poor Arthur anxiously. Having never seen him otherwise than in his town clothes she had no idea what he would look like. It had been left to the professor to help his ladies out of the boat because Renouard, as if intent on giving directions, had stepped forward at once to meet the half-caste Luiz hurrying down the path. In the distance, in front of the dazzlingly sunlit bungalow, a row of dark-faced house-boys unequal in stature and varied in complexion preserved the immobility of a guard of honour.

Luiz had taken off his soft felt hat before coming within earshot. Renouard bent his head to his rapid talk of domestic arrangements he meant to make for the visitors; another bed in the master's room for the ladies and a cot for the gentleman to be hung in the room opposite where - where Mr. Walter - here he gave a scared look all round - Mr. Walter - had died.

" Very good," assented Renouard in an even undertone.

"And remember what you have to say of him."

"Yes, master. Only" - he wriggled slightly and put one bare foot on the other for a moment in apologetic embarrassment - "only I - I - don't like to say it."

Renouard looked at him without anger, without any sort of expression. "Frightened of the dead? Eh? Well - all right. I will say it myself - I suppose once for all. Immediately he raised his voice very much.

"Send the boys down to bring up the luggage."

"Yes, master."

Renouard turned to his distinguished guests who, like a personally conducted party of tourists, had stopped and were looking about them.

"I am sorry," he began with an impassive face. "My man has just told me that Mr. Walter . . ." he managed to smile, but didn't correct himself . . . "has gone in a trading schooner on a short tour of the islands, to the westward."

This communication was received in profound silence.

Renouard forgot himself in the thought: "It's done!" But the sight of the string of boys marching up to the house with suit-cases and dressing-bags rescued him from that appalling abstraction.

"All I can do is to beg you to make yourselves at home with what patience you may."

This was so obviously the only thing to do that

everybody moved on at once. The professor walked alongside Renouard, behind the two ladies.

"Rather unexpected - this absence."

"Not exactly," muttered Renouard. "A trip has to be made every year to engage labour."

"I see . . . And he . . . How vexingly elusive the poor fellow has become! I'll begin to think that some wicked fairy is favouring this love tale with unpleasant attentions."

Renouard noticed that the party did not seem weighed down by this new disappointment. On the contrary they moved with a freer step. The professor's sister dropped her eye-glass to the end of its chain. Miss Moorsom took the lead. The professor, his lips unsealed, lingered in the open: but Renouard did not listen to that man's talk. He looked after that man's daughter - if indeed that creature of irresistible seductions were a daughter of mortals. The very intensity of his desire, as if his soul were streaming after her through his eyes, defeated his object of keeping hold of her as long as possible with, at least, one of his senses. Her moving outlines dissolved into a misty coloured shimmer of a woman made of flame and shadows, crossing the threshold of his house.

The days which followed were not exactly such as Renouard had feared - yet they were not better than his fears. They were accursed in all the moods they brought him. But the general aspect of things was quiet. The professor smoked innumerable pipes with the air of a worker on his holiday, always in movement and looking at things with that mysteriously sagacious aspect of men who are admittedly wiser than the rest of the world. His white head of hair - whiter than anything within the horizon except the broken water on the reefs - was glimpsed in every part of the plantation always on the move under the white parasol. And once he climbed the headland and appeared suddenly to those below, a white speck elevated in the blue, with a diminutive but statuesque effect.

Felicia Moorsom remained near the house. Sometimes she could be seen with a despairing expression scribbling rapidly in her lock-up dairy. But only for a moment. At the sound of Renouard's footsteps she would turn towards him her beautiful face, adorable in that calm which was like a wilful, like a cruel ignoring of her tremendous power. Whenever she sat on the verandah, on a chair more specially reserved for her use, Renouard would stroll up and sit on the steps near her, mostly silent, and often not trusting himself to turn his glance on her. She, very still with her eyes half-closed, looked down on his head - so that to a beholder (such as Professor Moorsom, for instance) she would appear to be turning over in her mind profound thoughts about that man sitting at her feet, his shoulders bowed a little, his hands listless - as if vanquished. And, indeed, the moral poison of falsehood has such a decomposing power that Renouard felt his old personality turn to dead dust. Often, in the evening, when they sat outside conversing languidly in the dark, he felt that he must rest his forehead on her feet and burst into tears.

The professor's sister suffered from some little strain caused by the unstability of her own feelings toward Renouard. She could not tell whether she really did dislike him or not. At times he appeared to her most fascinating; and, though he generally ended by saying something shockingly crude, she could not resist her inclination to talk with him - at least not always. One day when her niece had left them alone on the verandah she leaned forward in her chair - speckless, resplendent, and, in her way, almost as striking a personality as her niece, who did not resemble her in the least. "Dear Felicia has inherited her hair and the greatest part of her appearance from her mother," the maiden lady used to tell people.

She leaned forward then, confidentially.

"Oh! Mr. Renouard! Haven't you something comforting to say?"

He looked up, as surprised as if a voice from heaven had spoken with this perfect society intonation, and by the puzzled profundity of his blue eyes fluttered the wax-flower of refined womanhood. She continued. "For - I can speak to you openly on this tiresome subject - only think what a terrible strain this hope deferred must be for Felicia's heart - for her nerves."

"Why speak to me about it," he muttered feeling half choked suddenly.

"Why! As a friend - a well-wisher - the kindest of hosts. I am afraid we are really eating you out of house and home." She laughed a little. "Ah! When, when will this suspense be relieved! That poor lost Arthur! I confess that I am almost afraid of the great moment. It will be like seeing a ghost."

"Have you ever seen a ghost?" asked Renouard, in a dull voice.

She shifted her hands a little. Her pose was perfect in its ease and middle-aged grace.

"Not actually. Only in a photograph. But we have many friends who had the experience of apparitions."

"Ah! They see ghosts in London," mumbled Renouard, not looking at her.

"Frequently - in a certain very interesting set. But all sorts of people do. We have a friend, a very famous author - his ghost is a girl. One of my brother's intimates is a very great man of science. He is friendly with a ghost . . . Of a girl too," she added in a voice as if struck for the first time by the coincidence. "It is the photograph of that apparition which I have seen. Very sweet. Most interesting. A little cloudy naturally. . . . Mr. Renouard! I hope you are not a sceptic. It's so consoling to think. . ."

"Those plantation boys of mine see ghosts too," said Renouard grimly.

The sister of the philosopher sat up stiffly. What crudeness! It was always so with this strange young man.

"Mr. Renouard! How can you compare the superstitious fancies of your horrible savages with the manifestations . . . "

Words failed her. She broke off with a very faint primly angry smile. She was perhaps the more offended with him because of that flutter at the beginning of the conversation. And in a moment with perfect tact and dignity she got up from her chair and left him alone.

Renouard didn't even look up. It was not the displeasure of the lady which deprived him of his sleep that night. He was beginning to forget what simple, honest sleep was like. His hammock from the ship had been hung for him on a side verandah, and he spent his nights in it on his back, his hands folded on his chest, in a sort of half conscious, oppressed stupor. In the morning he watched with unseeing eyes the headland come out a shapeless inkblot against the thin light of the false dawn, pass through all the stages of daybreak to the deep purple of its outlined mass nimbed gloriously with the gold of the rising sun. He listened to the vague sounds of waking within the house: and suddenly he became aware of Luiz standing by the hammock - obviously troubled.

"What's the matter?"

"Tse! Tse! Tse!"

"Well, what now? Trouble with the boys?"

"No, master. The gentleman when I take him his bath water he speak to me. He ask me - he ask - when, when, I think Mr. Walter, he come back."

The half-caste's teeth chattered slightly. Renouard got out of the hammock.

"And he is here all the time - eh?"

Luiz nodded a scared affirmative, but at once protested, "I no see him. I never. Not I! The ignorant wild boys say they see . . .Something! Ough!"

He clapped his teeth on another short rattle, and stood there, shrunk, blighted, like a man in a freezing blast.

"And what did you say to the gentleman?"

"I say I don't know - and I clear out. I - I don't like to speak of him."

"All right. We shall try to lay that poor ghost," said Renouard gloomily, going off to a small hut near by to dress. He was saying to himself: "This fellow will end by giving me away. The last thing that I . . . No! That mustn't be." And feeling his hand being forced he discovered the whole extent of his cowardice.

CHAPTER X

That morning wandering about his plantation, more like a frightened soul than its creator and master, he dodged the white parasol bobbing up here and there like a buoy adrift on a sea of dark-green plants. The crop promised to be magnificent, and the fashionable philosopher of the age took other than a merely scientific interest in the experiment. His investments were judicious, but he had always some little money lying by, for experiments.

After lunch, being left alone with Renouard, he talked a little of cultivation and such matters. Then suddenly:

"By the way, is it true what my sister tells me, that your plantation boys have been disturbed by a ghost?"

Renouard, who since the ladies had left the table was not keeping such a strict watch on himself, came out of his abstraction with a start and a stiff smile.

"My foreman had some trouble with them during my absence. They funk working in a certain field on the slope of the hill."

"A ghost here!" exclaimed the amused professor. "Then our whole conception of the psychology of ghosts must be revised. This island has been uninhabited probably since the dawn of ages. How did a ghost come here. By air or water? And why did it leave its native haunts. Was it from misanthropy? Was he expelled from some community of spirits?"

Renouard essayed to respond in the same tone. The words died on his lips. Was it a man or a woman ghost, the professor inquired.

"I don't know." Renouard made an effort to appear at ease. He had, he said, a couple of Tahitian amongst his boys - a ghost-ridden race. They had started the scare. They had probably brought their ghost with them.

"Let us investigate the matter, Renouard," proposed the professor half in earnest. "We may make some interesting discoveries as to the state of primitive minds, at any rate."

This was too much. Renouard jumped up and leaving the room went out and walked about in front of the house. He would allow no one to force his hand. Presently the professor joined him outside. He carried his parasol, but had neither his book nor his pipe with him. Amiably serious he laid his hand on his "dear young friend's" arm.

"We are all of us a little strung up," he said. "For my part I have been like sister Anne in the story. But I cannot see anything coming. Anything that would be the least good for anybody - I mean."

Renouard had recovered sufficiently to murmur coldly his regret of this waste of time. For that was what, he supposed, the professor had in his mind.

"Time," mused Professor Moorsom. "I don't know that time can be wasted. But I will tell you, my dear friend, what this is: it is an awful waste of life. I mean for all of us. Even for my sister, who has got a headache and is gone to lie down."

He shook gently Renouard's arm. "Yes, for all of us! One may meditate on life endlessly, one may even have a poor opinion of it-but the fact remains that we have only one life to live. And it is short. Think of that, my young friend."

He released Renouard's arm and stepped out of the shade opening his parasol. It was clear that there was something more in his mind than mere anxiety about the date of his lectures for fashionable audiences. What did the man mean by his confounded platitudes? To Renouard, scared by Luiz in the morning (for he felt that nothing could be more fatal than to have his deception unveiled otherwise than by personal confession), this talk sounded like encouragement or a warning from that man who seemed to him to be very brazen and very subtle. It was like being bullied by the dead and cajoled by the living into a throw of dice for a supreme stake.

Renouard went away to some distance from the house and threw himself down in the shade of a tree. He lay there perfectly still with his forehead resting on his folded arms, light-headed and thinking. It seemed to him that he must be on fire, then that he had fallen into a cool whirlpool, a smooth funnel of water swirling about with nauseating rapidity. And then (it must have been a reminiscence of his boyhood) he was walking on the dangerous thin ice of a river, unable to turn back. . . . Suddenly it parted from shore to shore with a loud crack like the report of a gun.

With one leap he found himself on his feet. All was peace, stillness, sunshine. He walked away from there slowly. Had he been a gambler he would have perhaps been supported in a measure by the mere excitement. But he was not a gambler. He had always disdained that artificial manner of challenging the fates. The bungalow came into view, bright and pretty, and all about everything was peace, stillness, sunshine. . . .

While he was plodding towards it he had a disagreeable sense of the dead man's company at his elbow. The ghost! He seemed to be everywhere but in his grave. Could one ever shake him off? He wondered. At that moment Miss Moorsom came out on the verandah; and at once, as if by a mystery of radiating waves, she roused a great tumult in his heart, shook earth and sky together - but he plodded on. Then like a grave song-note in the storm her voice came to him ominously.

"Ah! Mr. Renouard. . . " He came up and smiled, but she was very serious. "I can't keep still any longer. Is there time to walk up this headland and back before dark?"

The shadows were lying lengthened on the ground; all was stillness and peace. "No," said Renouard, feeling suddenly as steady as a rock. "But I can show you a view from the central hill which your father has not seen. A view of reefs and of broken water without end, and of great wheeling clouds of sea-birds."

She came down the verandah steps at once and they moved off. "You go first," he proposed, "and I'll direct you. To the left."

She was wearing a short nankin skirt, a muslin blouse;
he could see through the thin stuff the skin of her
shoulders, of her arms. The noble delicacy of her neck
caused him a sort of transport. "The path begins where
these three palms are. The only palms on the island."

"I see."

She never turned her head. After a while she observed:
"This path looks as if it had been made recently."

"Quite recently," he assented very low.

They went on climbing steadily without exchanging
another word; and when they stood on the top she
gazed a long time before her. The low evening mist
veiled the further limit of the reefs. Above the
enormous and melancholy confusion, as of a fleet of
wrecked islands, the restless myriads of sea-birds
rolled and unrolled dark ribbons on the sky, gathered
in clouds, soared and stooped like a play of shadows,
for they were too far for them to hear their cries.

Renouard broke the silence in low tones.

"They'll be settling for the night presently." She made
no sound. Round them all was peace and declining
sunshine. Near by, the topmost pinnacle of Malata,
resembling the top of a buried tower, rose a rock,
weather-worn, grey, weary of watching the monotonous centuries of the Pacific. Renouard leaned his
shoulders against it. Felicia Moorsom faced him
suddenly, her splendid black eyes full on his face as
though she had made up her mind at last to destroy his

wits once and for all. Dazzled, he lowered his eyelids slowly.

"Mr. Renouard! There is something strange in all this. Tell me where he is?"

He answered deliberately.

"On the other side of this rock. I buried him there myself."

She pressed her hands to her breast, struggled for her breath for a moment, then: "Ohhh! . . . You buried him! . . . What sort of man are you? . . . You dared not tell! . . . He is another of your victims? . . . You dared not confess that evening. . . . You must have killed him. What could he have done to you? . . . You fastened on him some atrocious quarrel and . . ."

Her vengeful aspect, her poignant cries left him as unmoved as the weary rock against which he leaned. He only raised his eyelids to look at her and lowered them slowly. Nothing more. It silenced her. And as if ashamed she made a gesture with her hand, putting away from her that thought. He spoke, quietly ironic at first.

"Ha! the legendary Renouard of sensitive idiots - the ruthless adventurer - the ogre with a future. That was a parrot cry, Miss Moorsom. I don't think that the greatest fool of them all ever dared hint such a stupid thing of me that I killed men for nothing. No, I had noticed this man in a hotel. He had come from up country I was told, and was doing nothing. I saw him sitting there lonely in a corner like a sick crow, and I went over one evening to talk to him. Just on impulse.

He wasn't impressive. He was pitiful. My worst enemy could have told you he wasn't good enough to be one of Renouard's victims. It didn't take me long to judge that he was drugging himself. Not drinking. Drugs."

"Ah! It's now that you are trying to murder him," she cried.

"Really. Always the Renouard of shopkeepers' legend. Listen! I would never have been jealous of him. And yet I am jealous of the air you breathe, of the soil you tread on, of the world that sees you - moving free - not mine. But never mind. I rather liked him. For a certain reason I proposed he should come to be my assistant here. He said he believed this would save him. It did not save him from death. It came to him as it were from nothing - just a fall. A mere slip and tumble of ten feet into a ravine. But it seems he had been hurt before up-country - by a horse. He ailed and ailed. No, he was not a steel-tipped man. And his poor soul seemed to have been damaged too. It gave way very soon."

"This is tragic!" Felicia Moorsom whispered with feeling. Renouard's lips twitched, but his level voice continued mercilessly.

"That's the story. He rallied a little one night and said he wanted to tell me something. I, being a gentleman, he said, he could confide in me. I told him that he was mistaken. That there was a good deal of a plebeian in me, that he couldn't know. He seemed disappointed. He muttered something about his innocence and something that sounded like a curse on some woman, then turned to the wall and - just grew cold."

"On a woman," cried Miss Moorsom indignantly. "What woman?"

"I wonder!" said Renouard, raising his eyes and noting the crimson of her ear-lobes against the live whiteness of her complexion, the sombre, as if secret, night-splendour of her eyes under the writhing flames of her hair. "Some woman who wouldn't believe in that poor innocence of his. . . Yes. You probably. And now you will not believe in me - not even in me who must in truth be what I am - even to death. No! You won't. And yet, Felicia, a woman like you and a man like me do not often come together on this earth."

The flame of her glorious head scorched his face. He flung his hat far away, and his suddenly lowered eyelids brought out startlingly his resemblance to antique bronze, the profile of Pallas, still, austere, bowed a little in the shadow of the rock. "Oh! If you could only understand the truth that is in me!" he added.

She waited, as if too astounded to speak, till he looked up again, and then with unnatural force as if defending herself from some unspoken aspersion, "It's I who stand for truth here! Believe in you! In you, who by a heartless falsehood - and nothing else, nothing else, do you hear? - have brought me here, deceived, cheated, as in some abominable farce!" She sat down on a boulder, rested her chin in her hands, in the pose of simple grief - mourning for herself.

"It only wanted this. Why! Oh! Why is it that ugliness, ridicule, and baseness must fall across my path."

On that height, alone with the sky, they spoke to each

other as if the earth had fallen away from under their feet.

"Are you grieving for your dignity? He was a mediocre soul and could have given you but an unworthy existence."

She did not even smile at those words, but, superb, as if lifting a corner of the veil, she turned on him slowly.

"And do you imagine I would have devoted myself to him for such a purpose! Don't you know that reparation was due to him from me? A sacred debt - a fine duty. To redeem him would not have been in my power - I know it. But he was blameless, and it was for me to come forward. Don't you see that in the eyes of the world nothing could have rehabilitated him so completely as his marriage with me? No word of evil could be whispered of him after I had given him my hand. As to giving myself up to anything less than the shaping of a man's destiny - if I thought I could do it I would abhor myself. . . ." She spoke with authority in her deep fascinating, unemotional voice. Renouard meditated, gloomy, as if over some sinister riddle of a beautiful sphinx met on the wild road of his life.

"Yes. Your father was right. You are one of these aristocrats . . ."

She drew herself up haughtily.

"What do you say? My father! . . . I an aristocrat."

"Oh! I don't mean that you are like the men and women of the time of armours, castles, and great deeds. Oh, no! They stood on the naked soil, had traditions to be faithful to, had their feet on this earth of passions and death which is not a hothouse. They would have been too plebeian for you since they had to lead, to suffer with, to understand the commonest humanity. No, you are merely of the topmost layer, disdainful and superior, the mere pure froth and bubble on the inscrutable depths which some day will toss you out of existence. But you are you! You are you! You are the eternal love itself - only, O Divinity, it isn't your body, it is your soul that is made of foam."

She listened as if in a dream. He had succeeded so well in his effort to drive back the flood of his passion that his life itself seemed to run with it out of his body. At that moment he felt as one dead speaking. But the headlong wave returning with tenfold force flung him on her suddenly, with open arms and blazing eyes. She found herself like a feather in his grasp, helpless, unable to struggle, with her feet off the ground. But this contact with her, maddening like too much felicity, destroyed its own end. Fire ran through his veins, turned his passion to ashes, burnt him out and left him empty, without force - almost without desire. He let her go before she could cry out. And she was so used to the forms of repression enveloping, softening the crude impulses of old humanity that she no longer believed in their existence as if it were an exploded legend. She did not recognise what had happened to her. She came safe out of his arms, without a struggle, not even having felt afraid.

"What's the meaning of this?" she said, outraged but calm in a scornful way.

He got down on his knees in silence, bent low to her very feet, while she looked down at him, a little surprised, without animosity, as if merely curious to see what he would do. Then, while he remained bowed to the ground pressing the hem of her skirt to his lips, she made a slight movement. He got up.

"No," he said. "Were you ever so much mine what could I do with you without your consent? No. You don't conquer a wraith, cold mist, stuff of dreams, illusion. It must come to you and cling to your breast. And then! Oh! And then!"

All ecstasy, all expression went out of his face.

"Mr. Renouard," she said, "though you can have no claim on my consideration after having decoyed me here for the vile purpose, apparently, of gloating over me as your possible prey, I will tell you that I am not perhaps the extraordinary being you think I am. You may believe me. Here I stand for truth itself."

"What's that to me what you are?" he answered. "At a sign from you I would climb up to the seventh heaven to bring you down to earth for my own - and if I saw you steeped to the lips in vice, in crime, in mud, I would go after you, take you to my arms - wear you for an incomparable jewel on my breast. And that's love - true love - the gift and the curse of the gods. There is no other."

The truth vibrating in his voice made her recoil slightly, for she was not fit to hear it - not even a little - not even one single time in her life. It was revolting to her; and in her trouble, perhaps prompted by the suggestion of his name or to soften the harshness of expression, for she was obscurely moved, she spoke to him in French.

"Assez! J'ai horreur de tout cela," she said.

He was white to his very lips, but he was trembling no more. The dice had been cast, and not even violence could alter the throw. She passed by him unbendingly, and he followed her down the path. After a time she heard him saying:

"And your dream is to influence a human destiny?"

"Yes!" she answered curtly, unabashed, with a woman's complete assurance.

"Then you may rest content. You have done it."

She shrugged her shoulders slightly. But just before reaching the end of the path she relented, stopped, and went back to him.

"I don't suppose you are very anxious for people to know how near you came to absolute turpitude. You may rest easy on that point. I shall speak to my father, of course, and we will agree to say that he has died - nothing more."

"Yes," said Renouard in a lifeless voice. "He is dead. His very ghost shall be done with presently."

She went on, but he remained standing stock still in the dusk. She had already reached the three palms when she heard behind her a loud peal of laughter, cynical and joyless, such as is heard in smoking-rooms at the end of a scandalous story. It made her feel positively faint for a moment.

CHAPTER XI

Slowly a complete darkness enveloped Geoffrey Renouard. His resolution had failed him. Instead of following Felicia into the house, he had stopped under the three palms, and leaning against a smooth trunk had abandoned himself to a sense of an immense deception and the feeling of extreme fatigue. This walk up the hill and down again was like the supreme effort of an explorer trying to penetrate the interior of an unknown country, the secret of which is too well defended by its cruel and barren nature. Decoyed by a mirage, he had gone too far - so far that there was no going back. His strength was at an end. For the first time in his life he had to give up, and with a sort of despairing self-possession he tried to understand the cause of the defeat. He did not ascribe it to that absurd dead man.

The hesitating shadow of Luiz approached him unnoticed till it spoke timidly. Renouard started.

"Eh? What? Dinner waiting? You must say I beg to be excused. I can't come. But I shall see them to-morrow morning, at the landing place. Take your orders from the professor as to the sailing of the schooner. Go now."

Luiz , dumbfounded , retreated into the darkness.

Joseph Conrad

Renouard did not move, but hours afterwards, like the bitter fruit of his immobility, the words: "I had nothing to offer to her vanity," came from his lips in the silence of the island. And it was then only that he stirred, only to wear the night out in restless tramping up and down the various paths of the plantation. Luiz, whose sleep was made light by the consciousness of some impending change, heard footsteps passing by his hut, the firm tread of the master; and turning on his mats emitted a faint Tse! Tse! Tse! Of deep concern.

Lights had been burning in the bungalow almost all through the night; and with the first sign of day began the bustle of departure. House boys walked processionally carrying suit-cases and dressing-bags down to the schooner's boat, which came to the landing place at the bottom of the garden. Just as the rising sun threw its golden nimbus around the purple shape of the headland, the Planter of Malata was perceived pacing bare-headed the curve of the little bay. He exchanged a few words with the sailing-master of the schooner, then remained by the boat, standing very upright, his eyes on the ground, waiting.

He had not long to wait. Into the cool, overshadowed garden the professor descended first, and came jauntily down the path in a lively cracking of small shells. With his closed parasol hooked on his forearm, and a book in his hand, he resembled a banal tourist more than was permissible to a man of his unique distinction. He waved the disengaged arm from a distance, but at close quarters, arrested before Renouard's immobility, he made no offer to shake hands. He seemed to appraise the aspect of the man with a sharp glance, and made up his mind.

"We are going back by Suez," he began almost boisterously. "I have been looking up the sailing lists. If the zephirs of your Pacific are only moderately propitious I think we are sure to catch the mail boat due in Marseilles on the 18th of March. This will suit me excellently. . . ." He lowered his tone. "My dear young friend, I'm deeply grateful to you."

Renouard's set lips moved.

"Why are you grateful to me?"

"Ah! Why? In the first place you might have made us miss the next boat, mightn't you? . . . I don't thank you for your hospitality. You can't be angry with me for saying that I am truly thankful to escape from it. But I am grateful to you for what you have done, and - for being what you are."

It was difficult to define the flavour of that speech, but Renouard received it with an austerely equivocal smile. The professor stepping into the boat opened his parasol and sat down in the stern-sheets waiting for the ladies. No sound of human voice broke the fresh silence of the morning while they walked the broad path, Miss Moorsom a little in advance of her aunt.

When she came abreast of him Renouard raised his head.

"Good-bye, Mr. Renouard," she said in a low voice, meaning to pass on; but there was such a look of entreaty in the blue gleam of his sunken eyes that after an imperceptible hesitation she laid her hand, which was ungloved, in his extended palm.

"Will you condescend to remember me?" he asked, while an emotion with which she was angry made her pale cheeks flush and her black eyes sparkle.

"This is a strange request for you to make," she said exaggerating the coldness of her tone.

"Is it? Impudent perhaps. Yet I am not so guilty as you think; and bear in mind that to me you can never make reparation."

"Reparation? To you! It is you who can offer me no reparation for the offence against my feelings - and my person; for what reparation can be adequate for your odious and ridiculous plot so scornful in its implication, so humiliating to my pride. No! I don't want to remember you."

Unexpectedly, with a tightening grip, he pulled her nearer to him, and looking into her eyes with fearless despair -

"You'll have to. I shall haunt you," he said firmly.

Her hand was wrenched out of his grasp before he had time to release it. Felicia Moorsom stepped into the boat, sat down by the side of her father, and breathed tenderly on her crushed fingers.

The professor gave her a sidelong look - nothing more. But the professor's sister, yet on shore, had put up her long-handle double eye-glass to look at the scene. She dropped it with a faint rattle.

"I've never in my life heard anything so crude said to a lady," she murmured, passing before Renouard with a perfectly erect head. When, a moment afterwards, softening suddenly, she turned to throw a good-bye to that young man, she saw only his back in the distance moving towards the bungalow. She watched him go in - amazed - before she too left the soil of Malata.

Nobody disturbed Renouard in that room where he had shut himself in to breathe the evanescent perfume of her who for him was no more, till late in the afternoon when the half-caste was heard on the other side of the door.

He wanted the master to know that the trader Janet was just entering the cove.

Renouard's strong voice on his side of the door gave him most unexpected instructions. He was to pay off the boys with the cash in the office and arrange with the captain of the Janet to take every worker away from Malata, returning them to their respective homes. An order on the Dunster firm would be given to him in payment.

And again the silence of the bungalow remained unbroken till, next morning, the half-caste came to report that everything was done. The plantation boys were embarking now.

Through a crack in the door a hand thrust at him a piece of paper, and the door slammed to so sharply that Luiz stepped back. Then approaching cringingly the keyhole, in a propitiatory tone he asked:

"Do I go too, master?"

"Yes. You too. Everybody."

"Master stop here alone?"

Silence. And the half-caste's eyes grew wide with wonder. But he also, like those "ignorant savages," the plantation boys, was only too glad to leave an island haunted by the ghost of a white man. He backed away noiselessly from the mysterious silence in the closed room, and only in the very doorway of the bungalow allowed himself to give vent to his feelings by a deprecatory and pained -

"Tse! Tse! Tse!"

CHAPTER XII

The Moorsoms did manage to catch the homeward mail boat all right, but had only twenty-four hours in town. Thus the sentimental Willie could not see very much of them. This did not prevent him afterwards from relating at great length, with manly tears in his eyes, how poor Miss Moorsom - the fashionable and clever beauty - found her betrothed in Malata only to see him die in her arms. Most people were deeply touched by the sad story. It was the talk of a good many days.

But the all-knowing Editor, Renouard's only friend and crony, wanted to know more than the rest of the world. From professional incontinence, perhaps, he thirsted for a full cup of harrowing detail. And when he noticed Renouard's schooner lying in port day after day he sought the sailing master to learn the reason. The man told him that such were his instructions. He had been ordered to lie there a month before returning to Malata. And the month was nearly up. "I will ask you to give me a passage," said the Editor.

He landed in the morning at the bottom of the garden and found peace, stillness, sunshine reigning every-where, the doors and windows of the bungalow standing wide open, no sight of a human being anywhere, the plants growing rank and tall on the deserted fields. For hours the Editor and the schooner's crew, excited by the mystery, roamed over the island shouting Renouard's name; and at last set themselves in grim silence to explore systematically the uncleared bush and the deeper ravines in search of his corpse. What had happened? Had he been murdered by the boys? Or had he simply, capricious and secretive, abandoned his plantation taking the people with him. It was impossible to tell what had happened. At last, towards the decline of the day, the Editor and the sailing master discovered a track of sandals crossing a strip of sandy beach on the north shore of the bay. Following this track fearfully, they passed round the spur of the headland, and there on a large stone found the sandals, Renouard's white jacket, and the Malay sarong of chequered pattern which the planter of Malata was well known to wear when going to bathe. These things made a little heap, and the sailor remarked, after gazing at it in silence -

"Birds have been hovering over this for many a day."

"He's gone bathing and got drowned," cried the Editor in dismay.

"I doubt it, sir. If he had been drowned anywhere within a mile from the shore the body would have been washed out on the reefs. And our boats have found nothing so far."

Nothing was ever found - and Renouard's disappearance remained in the main inexplicable. For to whom could it have occurred that a man would set out calmly to swim beyond the confines of life - with a steady stroke - his eyes fixed on a star!

Next evening, from the receding schooner, the Editor looked back for the last time at the deserted island. A black cloud hung listlessly over the high rock on the middle hill; and under the mysterious silence of that shadow Malata lay mournful, with an air of anguish in the wild sunset, as if remembering the heart that was broken there.

Dec. 1913.

Joseph Conrad

THE PARTNER

"And that be hanged for a silly yarn. The boatmen here in Westport have been telling this lie to the summer visitors for years. The sort that gets taken out for a row at a shilling a head - and asks foolish questions - must be told something to pass the time away. D'ye know anything more silly than being pulled in a boat along a beach? . . . It's like drinking weak lemonade when you aren't thirsty. I don't know why they do it! They don't even get sick."

A forgotten glass of beer stood at his elbow; the locality was a small respectable smoking-room of a small respectable hotel, and a taste for forming chance acquaintances accounts for my sitting up late with him. His great, flat, furrowed cheeks were shaven; a thick, square wisp of white hairs hung from his chin; its waggling gave additional point to his deep utterance; and his general contempt for mankind with its activities and moralities was expressed in the rakish set of his big soft hat of black felt with a large rim, which he kept always on his head.

His appearance was that of an old adventurer, retired after many unholy experiences in the darkest parts of the earth; but I had every reason to believe that he had never been outside England. From a casual remark somebody dropped I gathered that in his early days he must have been somehow connected with shipping - with ships in docks. Of individuality he had plenty. And it was this which attracted my attention at first. But he was not easy to classify, and before the end of the week I gave him up with the vague definition, "an imposing old ruffian."

One rainy afternoon, oppressed by infinite boredom, I went into the smoking-room. He was sitting there in absolute immobility, which was really fakir-like and impressive. I began to wonder what could be the associations of that sort of man, his "milieu," his private connections, his views, his morality, his friends, and even his wife - when to my surprise he opened a conversation in a deep, muttering voice.

I must say that since he had learned from somebody that I was a writer of stories he had been acknowledging my existence by means of some vague growls in the morning.

He was essentially a taciturn man. There was an effect of rudeness in his fragmentary sentences. It was some time before I discovered that what he would be at was the process by which stories - stories for periodicals - were produced.

What could one say to a fellow like that? But I was bored to death; the weather continued impossible; and I resolved to be amiable.

"And so you make these tales up on your own. How do they ever come into your head?" he rumbled.

I explained that one generally got a hint for a tale.

"What sort of hint?"

"Well, for instance," I said, "I got myself rowed out to the rocks the other day. My boatman told me of the wreck on these rocks nearly twenty years ago. That could be used as a hint for a mainly descriptive bit of story with some such title as 'In the Channel,' for instance."

It was then that he flew out at the boatmen and the summer visitors who listen to their tales. Without moving a muscle of his face he emitted a powerful "Rot," from somewhere out of the depths of his chest, and went on in his hoarse, fragmentary mumble. "Stare at the silly rocks - nod their silly heads [the visitors, I presume]. What do they think a man is - blown-out paper bag or what? - go off pop like that when he's hit - Damn silly yarn - Hint indeed! . . . A lie?"

You must imagine this statuesque ruffian enhaloed in the black rim of his hat, letting all this out as an old dog growls sometimes, with his head up and staring-away eyes.

"Indeed!" I exclaimed. "Well, but even if untrue it IS a hint, enabling me to see these rocks, this gale they speak of, the heavy seas, etc., etc., in relation to mankind. The struggle against natural forces and the effect of the issue on at least one, say, exalted - "

He interrupted me by an aggressive -

"Would truth be any good to you?"

"I shouldn't like to say," I answered, cautiously. "It's said that truth is stranger than fiction."

"Who says that?" he mouthed.

"Oh! Nobody in particular."

I turned to the window; for the contemptuous beggar was oppressive to look at, with his immovable arm on the table. I suppose my unceremonious manner provoked him to a comparatively long speech.

"Did you ever see such a silly lot of rocks? Like plums in a slice of cold pudding."

I was looking at them - an acre or more of black dots scattered on the steel-grey shades of the level sea, under the uniform gossamer grey mist with a formless brighter patch in one place - the veiled whiteness of the cliff coming through, like a diffused, mysterious radiance. It was a delicate and wonderful picture, something expressive, suggestive, and desolate, a symphony in grey and black-a Whistler. But the next thing said by the voice behind me made me turn round. It growled out contempt for all associated notions of roaring seas with concise energy, then went on -

"I - no such foolishness - looking at the rocks out there - more likely call to mind an office - I used to look in sometimes at one time - office in London - one of them small streets behind Cannon Street Station. "

He was very deliberate; not jerky, only fragmentary; at times profane.

"That's a rather remote connection," I observed, approaching him.

"Connection? To Hades with your connections. It was an accident."

" Still , " I said , " an accident has its backward and forward connections , which , if they could be set forth - "

Without moving he seemed to lend an attentive ear.

"Aye! Set forth. That's perhaps what you could do. Couldn't you now? There's no sea life in this connection. But you can put it in out of your head - if you like."

"Yes. I could, if necessary," I said. "Sometimes it pays to put in a lot out of one's head, and sometimes it doesn't. I mean that the story isn't worth it. Everything's in that."

It amused me to talk to him like this. He reflected audibly that he guessed story-writers were out after money like the rest of the world which had to live by its wits: and that it was extraordinary how far people who were out after money would go. . . Some of them.

Then he made a sally against sea life. Silly sort of life, he called it. No opportunities, no experience, no variety, nothing. Some fine men came out of it - he admitted - but no more chance in the world if put to it than fly. Kids. So Captain Harry Dunbar. Good sailor. Great name as a skipper. Big man; short side-whiskers going grey, fine face, loud voice. A good fellow, but no more up to people's tricks than a baby.

"That's the captain of the Sagamore you're talking about," I said, confidently.

After a low, scornful "Of course" he seemed now to hold on the wall with his fixed stare the vision of that city office, "at the back of Cannon Street Station," while he growled and mouthed a fragmentary description, jerking his chin up now and then, as if angry.

It was, according to his account, a modest place of business, not shady in any sense, but out of the way, in a small street now rebuilt from end to end. "Seven doors from the Cheshire Cat public house under the railway bridge. I used to take my lunch there when my business called me to the city. Cloete would come in to have his chop and make the girl laugh. No need to talk much, either, for that. Nothing but the way he would twinkle his spectacles on you and give a twitch of his thick mouth was enough to start you off before he began one of his little tales. Funny fellow, Cloete. C-l-o-e-t-e - Cloete."

"What was he - a Dutchman?" I asked, not seeing in the least what all this had to do with the Westport boatmen and the Westport summer visitors and this extraordinary old fellow's irritable view of them as liars and fools. "Devil knows," he grunted, his eyes on the wall as if not to miss a single movement of a cinematograph picture. "Spoke nothing but English, anyway. First I saw him - comes off a ship in dock from the States - passenger. Asks me for a small hotel near by. Wanted to be quiet and have a look round for a few days. I took him to a place - friend of mine. . . Next time - in the City - Hallo! You're very obliging - have a drink. Talks plenty about himself. Been years in the States. All sorts of business all over the place. With some patent medicine people, too. Travels. Writes advertisements and all that. Tells me funny stories.

Tall, loose-limbed fellow. Black hair up on end, like a brush; long face, long legs, long arms, twinkle in his specs , jocular way of speaking - in a low voice. See that?"

I nodded, but he was not looking at me.

"Never laughed so much in my life. The beggar - would make you laugh telling you how he skinned his own father. He was up to that, too. A man who's been in the patent-medicine trade will be up to anything from pitch-and-toss to wilful murder. And that's a bit of hard truth for you. Don't mind what they do - think they can carry off anything and talk themselves out of anything - all the world's a fool to them. Business man, too, Cloete. Came over with a few hundred pounds. Looking for something to do - in a quiet way. Nothing like the old country, after all, says he. . . And so we part - I with more drinks in me than I was used to. After a time, perhaps six months or so, I run up against him again in Mr. George Dunbar's office. Yes, THAT office. It wasn't often that I . . .However, there was a bit of his cargo in a ship in dock that I wanted to ask Mr. George about. In comes Cloete out of the room at the back with some papers in his hand. Partner. You understand?"

"Aha!" I said. "The few hundred pounds."

"And that tongue of his," he growled. "Don't forget that tongue. Some of his tales must have opened George Dunbar's eyes a bit as to what business means."

"A plausible fellow," I suggested.

"H'm! You must have it in your own way - of course.

Well. Partner. George Dunbar puts his top-hat on and tells me to wait a moment. . . George always looked as though he were making a few thousands a year - a city swell. . . Come along, old man! And he and Captain Harry go out together - some business with a solicitor round the corner. Captain Harry, when he was in England, used to turn up in his brother's office regularly about twelve. Sat in a corner like a good boy, reading the paper and smoking his pipe. So they go out. . . Model brothers, says Cloete - two love-birds - I am looking after the tinned-fruit side of this cozy little show. . .Gives me that sort of talk. Then by-and-by: What sort of old thing is that Sagamore? Finest ship out - eh? I dare say all ships are fine to you. You live by them. I tell you what; I would just as soon put my money into an old stocking. Sooner!"

He drew a breath, and I noticed his hand, lying loosely on the table, close slowly into a fist. In that immovable man it was startling, ominous, like the famed nod of the Commander.

"So, already at that time - note - already," he growled.

"But hold on," I interrupted. "The Sagamore belonged to Mundy and Rogers, I've been told."

He snorted contemptuously. "Damn boatmen - know no better. Flew the firm's HOUSE-FLAG. That's another thing. Favour. It was like this: When old man Dunbar died, Captain Harry was already in command with the firm. George chucked the bank he was clerking in-to go on his own with what there was to share after the old chap. George was a smart man. Started warehousing; then two or three things at a time: wood-pulp, preserved-fruit trade, and so on. And

Captain Harry let him have his share to work with. . . I am provided for in my ship, he says. . . But by-and-by Mundy and Rogers begin to sell out to foreigners all their ships - go into steam right away. Captain Harry gets very upset - lose command, part with the ship he was fond of - very wretched. Just then, so it happened, the brothers came in for some money - an old woman died or something. Quite a tidy bit. Then young George says: There's enough between us two to buy the Sagamore with. . . But you'll need more money for your business, cries Captain Harry - and the other laughs at him: My business is going on all right. Why, I can go out and make a handful of sovereigns while you are trying to get your pipe to draw, old man. . . Mundy and Rogers very friendly about it: Certainly, Captain. And we will manage her for you, if you like, as if she were still our own. . . Why, with a connection like that it was good investment to buy that ship. Good! Aye, at the time."

The turning of his head slightly toward me at this point was like a sign of strong feeling in any other man.

"You'll mind that this was long before Cloete came into it at all," he muttered, warningly.

"Yes. I will mind," I said. "We generally say: some years passed. That's soon done."

He eyed me for a while silently in an unseeing way, as if engrossed in the thought of the years so easily dealt with; his own years, too, they were, the years before and the years (not so many) after Cloete came upon the scene. When he began to speak again, I discerned his intention to point out to me, in his obscure and graphic manner, the influence on George Dunbar of long association with Cloete's easy moral standards, unscrupulously persuasive gift of humour (funny fellow), and adventurously reckless disposition. He desired me anxiously to elaborate this view, and I assured him it was quite within my powers. He wished me also to understand that George's business had its ups and downs (the other brother was meantime sailing to and fro serenely); that he got into low water at times, which worried him rather, because he had married a young wife with expensive tastes. He was having a pretty anxious time of it generally; and just then Cloete ran up in the city somewhere against a man working a patent medicine (the fellow's old trade) with some success, but which, with capital, capital to the tune of thousands to be spent with both hands on advertising, could be turned into a great thing - infinitely better - paying than a gold-mine. Cloete became excited at the possibilities of that sort of business, in which he was an expert. I understood that George's partner was all on fire from the contact with this unique opportunity.

"So he goes in every day into George's room about eleven, and sings that tune till George gnashes his teeth with rage. Do shut up. What's the good? No money. Hardly any to go on with, let alone pouring thousands into advertising. Never dare propose to his brother Harry to sell the ship. Couldn't think of it. Worry him to death. It would be like the end of the world coming. And certainly not for a business of that kind! . . . Do you think it would be a swindle? asks Cloete, twitching his mouth. . . George owns up: No-would be no better than a squeamish ass if he thought that, after all these years in business.

"Cloete looks at him hard - Never thought of

SELLING the ship. Expected the blamed old thing wouldn't fetch half her insured value by this time. Then George flies out at him. What's the meaning, then, of these silly jeers at ship-owning for the last three weeks? Had enough of them, anyhow.

"Angry at having his mouth made to water, see. Cloete don't get excited. . . I am no squeamish ass, either, says he, very slowly. 'Tisn't selling your old Sagamore wants. The blamed thing wants tomahawking (seems the name Sagamore means an Indian chief or something. The figure-head was a half-naked savage with a feather over one ear and a hatchet in his belt). Tomahawking, says he.

"What do you mean? asks George. . . Wrecking - it could be managed with perfect safety, goes on Cloete - your brother would then put in his share of insurance money. Needn't tell him exactly what for. He thinks you're the smartest business man that ever lived. Make his fortune, too. . . George grips the desk with both hands in his rage. . . You think my brother's a man to cast away his ship on purpose. I wouldn't even dare think of such a thing in the same room with him - the finest fellow that ever lived. . . Don't make such noise; they'll hear you outside, says Cloete; and he tells him that his brother is the salted pattern of all virtues, but all that's necessary is to induce him to stay ashore for a voyage - for a holiday - take a rest - why not? . . . In fact, I have in view somebody up to that sort of game - Cloete whispers.

"George nearly chokes. . . So you think I am of that sort - you think ME capable - What do you take me for? . . . He almost loses his head, while Cloete keeps cool, only gets white about the gills. . . I take you for a

man who will be most cursedly hard up before long. . .
He goes to the door and sends away the clerks - there
were only two - to take their lunch hour. Comes back
What are you indignant about? Do I want you to rob
the widow and orphan? Why, man! Lloyd's a
corporation, it hasn't got a body to starve. There's forty
or more of them perhaps who underwrote the lines on
that silly ship of yours. Not one human being would go
hungry or cold for it. They take every risk into
consideration. Everything I tell you. . . That sort of
talk. H'm! George too upset to speak - only gurgles and
waves his arms; so sudden, you see. The other,
warming his back at the fire, goes on. Wood-pulp
business next door to a failure. Tinned-fruit trade
nearly played out. . .You're frightened, he says; but the
law is only meant to frighten fools away. . . And he
shows how safe casting away that ship would be.
Premiums paid for so many, many years. No shadow
of suspicion could arise. And, dash it all! a ship must
meet her end some day.

"I am not frightened. I am indignant," says George
Dunbar.

"Cloete boiling with rage inside. Chance of a lifetime -
his chance! And he says kindly: Your wife'll be much
more indignant when you ask her to get out of that
pretty house of yours and pile in into a two-pair back -
with kids perhaps, too. . .

"George had no children. Married a couple of years;
looked forward to a kid or two very much. Feels more
upset than ever. Talks about an honest man for father,
and so on. Cloete grins: You be quick before they
come, and they'll have a rich man for father, and no
one the worse for it. That's the beauty of the thing.

Joseph Conrad

"George nearly cries. I believe he did cry at odd times. This went on for weeks. He couldn't quarrel with Cloete. Couldn't pay off his few hundreds; and besides, he was used to have him about. Weak fellow, George. Cloete generous, too. . . Don't think of my little pile, says he. Of course it's gone when we have to shut up. But I don't care, he says. . . And then there was George's new wife. When Cloete dines there, the beggar puts on a dress suit; little woman liked it; . . . Mr. Cloete, my husband's partner; such a clever man, man of the world, so amusing! . . . When he dines there and they are alone: Oh, Mr. Cloete, I wish George would do something to improve our prospects. Our position is really so mediocre. . . And Cloete smiles, but isn't surprised, because he had put all these notions himself into her empty head. . . What your husband wants is enterprise, a little audacity. You can encourage him best, Mrs. Dunbar. . . She was a silly, extravagant little fool. Had made George take a house in Norwood. Live up to a lot of people better off than themselves. I saw her once; silk dress, pretty boots, all feathers and scent, pink face. More like the Promenade at the Alhambra than a decent home, it looked to me. But some women do get a devil of a hold on a man."

"Yes, some do," I assented. "Even when the man is the husband."

"My missis," he addressed me unexpectedly, in a solemn, surprisingly hollow tone, "could wind me round her little finger. I didn't find it out till she was gone. Aye. But she was a woman of sense, while that piece of goods ought to have been walking the streets, and that's all I can say. . . You must make her up out of your head. You will know the sort."

"Leave all that to me," I said.

"H'm!" he grunted, doubtfully, then going back to his scornful tone: "A month or so afterwards the Sagamore arrives home. All very jolly at first. . . Hallo, George boy! Hallo, Harry, old man! . . . But by and by Captain Harry thinks his clever brother is not looking very well. And George begins to look worse. He can't get rid of Cloete's notion. It has stuck in his head. . . There's nothing wrong - quite well. . . Captain Harry still anxious. Business going all right, eh? Quite right. Lots of business. Good business. . . Of course Captain Harry believes that easily. Starts chaffing his brother in his jolly way about rolling in money. George's shirt sticks to his back with perspiration, and he feels quite angry with the captain. . . The fool, he says to himself. Rolling in money, indeed! And then he thinks suddenly: Why not? . . . Because Cloete's notion has got hold of his mind.

"But next day he weakens and says to Cloete . . . Perhaps it would be best to sell. Couldn't you talk to my brother? and Cloete explains to him over again for the twentieth time why selling wouldn't do, anyhow. No! The Sagamore must be tomahawked - as he would call it; to spare George's feelings, maybe. But every time he says the word, George shudders. . . I've got a man at hand competent for the job who will do the trick for five hundred, and only too pleased at the chance, says Cloete. . . George shuts his eyes tight at that sort of talk - but at the same time he thinks: Humbug! There can be no such man. And yet if there was such a man it would be safe enough - perhaps.

"And Cloete always funny about it. He couldn't talk about anything without it seeming there was a great joke in it somewhere. . . Now, says he, I know you are a moral citizen, George. Morality is mostly funk, and I think you're the funkiest man I ever came across in my travels. Why, you are afraid to speak to your brother. Afraid to open your mouth to him with a fortune for us all in sight. . . George flares up at this: no, he ain't afraid; he will speak; bangs fist on the desk. And Cloete pats him on the back. . . We'll be made men presently, he says.

"But the first time George attempts to speak to Captain Harry his heart slides down into his boots. Captain Harry only laughs at the notion of staying ashore. He wants no holiday, not he. But Jane thinks of remaining in England this trip. Go about a bit and see some of her people. Jane was the Captain's wife; round-faced, pleasant lady. George gives up that time; but Cloete won't let him rest. So he tries again; and the Captain frowns. He frowns because he's puzzled. He can't make it out. He has no notion of living away from his Sagamore. . .

"Ah!" I cried. "Now I understand."

"No, you don't," he growled, his black, contemptuous stare turning on me crushingly.

"I beg your pardon," I murmured.

"H'm! Very well, then. Captain Harry looks very stern, and George crumples all up inside. . . He sees through me, he thinks. . . Of course it could not be; but George, by that time, was scared at his own shadow. He is shirking it with Cloete, too. Gives his partner to understand that his brother has half a mind to try a spell on shore, and so on. Cloete waits, gnawing his fingers; so anxious. Cloete really had found a man for the job. Believe it or not, he had found him inside the very boarding-house he lodged in - somewhere about Tottenham Court Road. He had noticed down-stairs a fellow - a boarder and not a boarder - hanging about the dark - part of the passage mostly; sort of 'man of the house,' a slinking chap. Black eyes. White face. The woman of the house - a widow lady, she called herself - very full of Mr. Stafford; Mr. Stafford this and Mr. Stafford that. . . Anyhow, Cloete one evening takes him out to have a drink. Cloete mostly passed away his evenings in saloon bars. No drunkard, though, Cloete; for company; liked to talk to all sorts there; just habit; American fashion.

"So Cloete takes that chap out more than once. Not very good company, though. Little to say for himself. Sits quiet and drinks what's given to him, eyes always half closed, speaks sort of demure. . . I've had misfortunes, he says. The truth was they had kicked him out of a big steam-ship company for disgraceful conduct; nothing to affect his certificate, you understand; and he had gone down quite easily. Liked it, I expect. Anything's better than work. Lived on the widow lady who kept that boarding-house."

"That's almost incredible," I ventured to interrupt. "A man with a master's certificate, do you mean?"

"I do; I've known them 'bus cads," he growled, contemptuously. "Yes. Swing on the tail-board by the strap and yell, 'tuppence all the way.' Through drink. But this Stafford was of another kind. Hell's full of such Staffords; Cloete would make fun of him, and then there would be a nasty gleam in the fellow's half-shut eye. But Cloete was generally kind to him. Cloete was a fellow that would be kind to a mangy dog. Anyhow, he used to stand drinks to that object, and now and then gave him half a crown - because the widow lady kept Mr. Stafford short of pocket-money. They had rows almost every day down in the basement. . .

It was the fellow being a sailor that put into Cloete's mind the first notion of doing away with the Sagamore. He studies him a bit, thinks there's enough devil in him yet to be tempted, and one evening he says to him . . . I suppose you wouldn't mind going to sea again, for a spell? . . . The other never raises his eyes; says it's scarcely worth one's while for the miserable salary one gets. . . Well, but what do you say to captain's wages for a time, and a couple of hundred extra if you are compelled to come home without the ship. Accidents will happen, says Cloete. . . Oh! sure to, says that Stafford; and goes on taking sips of his drink as if he had no interest in the matter.

"Cloete presses him a bit; but the other observes, impudent and languid like: You see, there's no future in a thing like that - is there? . . Oh! no, says Cloete. Certainly not. I don't mean this to have any future - as far as you are concerned. It's a 'once for all' transaction. Well, what do you estimate your future at? He asks. . . The fellow more listless than ever - nearly asleep. - I believe the skunk was really too lazy to care. Small cheating at cards, wheedling or bullying his living out of some woman or other, was more his style. Cloete swears at him in whispers something awful. All this in the saloon bar of the Horse Shoe, Tottenham Court Road. Finally they agree, over the second sixpennyworth of Scotch hot, on five hundred pounds as the price of tomahawking the Sagamore. And Cloete waits to see what George can do.

"A week or two goes by. The other fellow loafs about the house as if there had been nothing, and Cloete begins to doubt whether he really means ever to tackle that job. But one day he stops Cloete at the door, with his downcast eyes: What about that employment you wished to give me? he asks. . . You see, he had played some more than usual dirty trick on the woman and expected awful ructions presently; and to be fired out for sure. Cloete very pleased. George had been prevaricating to him such a lot that he really thought the thing was as well as settled. And he says: Yes. It's time I introduced you to my friend. Just get your hat and we will go now. . .

"The two come into the office, and George at his desk sits up in a sudden panic - staring. Sees a tallish fellow, sort of nasty-handsome face, heavy eyes, half shut; short drab overcoat, shabby bowler hat, very careful - like in his movements. And he thinks to himself, Is that how such a man looks! No, the thing's impossible. Cloete does the introduction, and the fellow turns round to look behind him at the chair before he sits down. . . A thoroughly competent man, Cloete goes on The man says nothing, sits perfectly quiet. And George can't speak, throat too dry. Then he makes an effort: H'm! H'm! Oh yes - unfortunately - sorry to disappoint - my brother - made other arrangements - going himself.

"The fellow gets up, never raising his eyes off the ground, like a modest girl, and goes out softly, right out of the office without a sound. Cloete sticks his chin in his hand and bites all his fingers at once. George's heart slows down and he speaks to Cloete. . . This can't be done. How can it be? Directly the ship is lost Harry would see through it. You know he is a man to go to the underwriters himself with his suspicions. And he would break his heart over me. How can I play that on him? There's only two of us in the world belonging to each other. . .

"Cloete lets out a horrid cuss-word, jumps up, bolts away into his room, and George hears him there banging things around. After a while he goes to the door and says in a trembling voice: You ask me for an impossibility. . . Cloete inside ready to fly out like a tiger and rend him; but he opens the door a little way and says softly: Talking of hearts, yours is no bigger than a mouse's, let me tell you. . . But George doesn't care - load off the heart, anyhow. And just then Captain Harry comes in. . . Hallo, George boy. I am little late. What about a chop at the Cheshire, now? Right you are, old man. . . And off they go to lunch together. Cloete has nothing to eat that day.

"George feels a new man for a time; but all of a sudden that fellow Stafford begins to hang about the street, in sight of the house door. The first time George sees him he thinks he made a mistake. But no; next time he has to go out, there is the very fellow skulking on the other side of the road. It makes George nervous; but he must go out on business, and when the fellow cuts across the road-way he dodges him. He dodges him once, twice, three times; but at last he gets nabbed in his very doorway. . . What do you want? he says, trying to look fierce.

"It seems that ructions had come in the basement of that boarding-house, and the widow lady had turned on him (being jealous mad), to the extent of talking of the police. THAT Mr. Stafford couldn't stand; so he cleared out like a scared stag, and there he was, chucked into the streets, so to speak. Cloete looked so savage as he went to and fro that he hadn't the spunk to tackle him; but George seemed a softer kind to his eye. He would have been glad of half a quid, anything. I've had misfortunes, he says softly, in his demure way, which frightens George more than a row would have done. . . Consider the severity of my disappointment, he says. . .

"George, instead of telling him to go to the devil, loses his head.. . I don't know you. What do you want? he cries, and bolts up-stairs to Cloete. . . . Look what's come of it, he gasps; now we are at the mercy of that horrid fellow. . . Cloete tries to show him that the fellow can do nothing; but George thinks that some sort of scandal may be forced on, anyhow. Says that he can't live with that horror haunting him. Cloete would laugh if he weren't too weary of it all. Then a thought strikes him and he changes his tune. . . Well, perhaps! I will go down-stairs and send him away to begin with. He comes back. . . He's gone. But perhaps you are right. The fellow's hard up, and that's what makes people desperate. The best thing would be to get him out of the country for a time. Look here, the poor devil is really in want of employment. I won't ask you much this time: only to hold your tongue; and I shall try to get your brother to take him as chief officer. At this George lays his arms and his head on his desk, so that Cloete feels sorry for him. But altogether Cloete feels more cheerful because he has shaken the ghost a bit into that Stafford. That very afternoon he buys him a suit of blue clothes, and tells him that he will have to turn to and work for his living now. Go to sea as mate of the Sagamore. The skunk wasn't very willing, but what with having nothing to eat and no place to sleep in, and the woman having frightened him with the talk of some prosecution or other, he had no choice, properly speaking. Cloete takes care of him for a couple of days. . . Our arrangement still stands, says he. Here's the ship bound for Port Elizabeth; not a safe anchorage at all. Should she by chance part from her anchors in a north-east gale and get lost on the beach, as many of them do, why, it's five hundred in your pocket - and a quick return home. You are up to the job, ain't you?

"Our Mr. Stafford takes it all in with downcast eyes. . . I am a competent seaman, he says, with his sly, modest air. A ship's chief mate has no doubt many opportunities to manipulate the chains and anchors to some purpose. . . At this Cloete thumps him on the back: You'll do, my noble sailor. Go in and win. . .

"Next thing George knows, his brother tells him that he had occasion to oblige his partner. And glad of it, too. Likes the partner no end. Took a friend of his as mate. Man had his troubles, been ashore a year nursing a dying wife, it seems. Down on his luck. . . George protests earnestly that he knows nothing of the person. Saw him once. Not very attractive to look at. . . And Captain Harry says in his hearty way, That's so, but must give the poor devil a chance. . .

"So Mr. Stafford joins in dock. And it seems that he did manage to monkey with one of the cables - keeping his mind on Port Elizabeth. The riggers had all the cable ranged on deck to clean lockers. The new mate watches them go ashore - dinner hour - and sends the ship-keeper out of the ship to fetch him a bottle of beer. Then he goes to work whittling away the forelock of the forty-five-fathom shackle-pin, gives it a tap or two with a hammer just to make it loose, and of course that cable wasn't safe any more. Riggers come back - you know what riggers are: come day, go day, and God send Sunday. Down goes the chain into the locker without their foreman looking at the shackles at all. What does he care? He ain't going in the ship. And two days later the ship goes to sea. . . "

At this point I was incautious enough to breathe out another "I see," which gave offence again, and brought on me a rude "No, you don't" - as before. But in the pause he remembered the glass of beer at his elbow. He drank half of it, wiped his mustaches, and remarked grimly -

"Don't you think that there will be any sea life in this, because there ain't. If you're going to put in any out of your own head, now's your chance. I suppose you know what ten days of bad weather in the Channel are like? I don't. Anyway, ten whole days go by. One Monday Cloete comes to the office a little late - hears a woman's voice in George's room and looks in. Newspapers on the desk, on the floor; Captain Harry's wife sitting with red eyes and a bag on the chair near her. . . Look at this, says George, in great excitement, showing him a paper. Cloete's heart gives a jump. Ha! Wreck in Westport Bay. The Sagamore gone ashore early hours of Sunday, and so the newspaper men had time to put in some of their work. Columns of it. Lifeboat out twice. Captain and crew remain by the ship. Tugs summoned to assist. If the weather improves, this well-known fine ship may yet be saved. You know the way these chaps put it. . . Mrs. Harry there on her way to catch a train from Cannon Street. Got an hour to wait.

" Cloete takes George aside and whispers: Ship saved yet! Oh, damn! That must never be; you hear? But George looks at him dazed, and Mrs. Harry keeps on sobbing quietly: . . . I ought to have been with him. But I am going to him. . . We are all going together, cries Cloete, all of a sudden. He rushes out, sends the woman a cup of hot bovril from the shop across the road, buys a rug for her, thinks of everything; and in the train tucks her in and keeps on talking, thirteen to the dozen, all the way, to keep her spirits up, as it were; but really because he can't hold his peace for very joy. Here's the thing done all at once, and nothing to pay. Done. Actually done. His head swims now and again when he thinks of it. What enormous luck! It almost frightens him. He would like to yell and sing. Meantime George Dunbar sits in his corner, looking so deadly miserable that at last poor Mrs. Harry tries to comfort him, and so cheers herself up at the same time by talking about how her Harry is a prudent man; not likely to risk his crew's life or his own unnecessarily - and so on.

"First thing they hear at Westport station is that the life-boat has been out to the ship again, and has brought off the second officer, who had hurt himself, and a few sailors. Captain and the rest of the crew, about fifteen in all, are still on board. Tugs expected to arrive every moment.

"They take Mrs. Harry to the inn, nearly opposite the rocks; she bolts straight up-stairs to look out of the window, and she lets out a great cry when she sees the wreck. She won't rest till she gets on board to her Harry. Cloete soothes her all he can. . . All right; you try to eat a mouthful, and we will go to make inquiries.

" He draws George out of the room: Look here, she can't go on board, but I shall. I'll see to it that he doesn't stop in the ship too long. Let's go and find the coxswain of the life-boat. . . George follows him, shivering from time to time. The waves are washing over the old pier; not much wind, a wild, gloomy sky over the bay. In the whole world only one tug away off, heading to the seas, tossed in and out of sight every minute as regular as clockwork.

"They meet the coxswain and he tells them: Yes! He's going out again. No, they ain't in danger on board - not yet. But the ship's chance is very poor. Still, if the wind doesn't pipe up again and the sea goes down something might be tried. After some talk he agrees to take Cloete on board; supposed to be with an urgent message from the owners to the captain.

"Whenever Cloete looks at the sky he feels comforted; it looks so threatening. George Dunbar follows him about with a white face and saying nothing. Cloete takes him to have a drink or two, and by and by he begins to pick up. . . That's better, says Cloete; dash me if it wasn't like walking about with a dead man before. You ought to be throwing up your cap, man. I feel as if I wanted to stand in the street and cheer. Your brother is safe, the ship is lost, and we are made men.

"Are you certain she's lost? asks George. It would be an awful blow after all the agonies I have gone through in my mind, since you first spoke to me, if she were to be got off - and - and - all this temptation to begin over again. . . For we had nothing to do with this; had we?

"Of course not, says Cloete. Wasn't your brother himself in charge? It's providential. . . Oh! cries

George, shocked. . . Well, say it's the devil, says Cloete, cheerfully. I don't mind! You had nothing to do with it any more than a baby unborn, you great softy, you. . . Cloete has got so that he almost loved George Dunbar. Well. Yes. That was so. I don't mean he respected him. He was just fond of his partner.

"They go back, you may say fairly skipping, to the hotel, and find the wife of the captain at the open window, with her eyes on the ship as if she wanted to fly across the bay over there. . . Now then, Mrs. Dunbar, cries Cloete, you can't go, but I am going. Any messages? Don't be shy. I'll deliver every word faithfully. And if you would like to give me a kiss for him, I'll deliver that too, dash me if I don't.

"He makes Mrs. Harry laugh with his patter. . . Oh, dear Mr. Cloete, you are a calm, reasonable man. Make him behave sensibly. He's a bit obstinate, you know, and he's so fond of the ship, too. Tell him I am here - looking on. . . Trust me, Mrs. Dunbar. Only shut that window, that's a good girl. You will be sure to catch cold if you don't, and the Captain won't be pleased coming off the wreck to find you coughing and sneezing so that you can't tell him how happy you are. And now if you can get me a bit of tape to fasten my glasses on good to my ears, I will be going. . .

"How he gets on board I don't know. All wet and shaken and excited and out of breath, he does get on board. Ship lying over, smothered in sprays, but not moving very much; just enough to jag one's nerve a bit. He finds them all crowded on the deck-house forward, in their shiny oilskins, with faces like sick men. Captain Harry can't believe his eyes. What! Mr. Cloete! What are you doing here, in God's name? . . .

Your wife's ashore there, looking on, gasps out Cloete; and after they had talked a bit, Captain Harry thinks it's uncommonly plucky and kind of his brother's partner to come off to him like this. Man glad to have somebody to talk to. . . It's a bad business, Mr. Cloete, he says. And Cloete rejoices to hear that. Captain Harry thinks he had done his best, but the cable had parted when he tried to anchor her. It was a great trial to lose the ship. Well, he would have to face it. He fetches a deep sigh now and then. Cloete almost sorry he had come on board, because to be on that wreck keeps his chest in a tight band all the time. They crouch out of the wind under the port boat, a little apart from the men. The life-boat had gone away after putting Cloete on board, but was coming back next high water to take off the crew if no attempt at getting the ship afloat could be made. Dusk was falling; winter's day; black sky; wind rising. Captain Harry felt melancholy. God's will be done. If she must be left on the rocks - why, she must. A man should take what God sends him standing up. . . Suddenly his voice breaks, and he squeezes Cloete's arm: It seems as if I couldn't leave her, he whispers. Cloete looks round at the men like a lot of huddled sheep and thinks to himself: They won't stay. . . Suddenly the ship lifts a little and sets down with a thump. Tide rising. Everybody beginning to look out for the life-boat. Some of the men made her out far away and also two more tugs. But the gale has come on again, and everybody knows that no tug will ever dare come near the ship.

"That's the end, Captain Harry says, very low. . . . Cloete thinks he never felt so cold in all his life. . . And I feel as if I didn't care to live on just now, mutters Captain Harry . . . Your wife's ashore, looking on, says

Cloete . . . Yes. Yes. It must be awful for her to look at the poor old ship lying here done for. Why, that's our home.

"Cloete thinks that as long as the Sagamore's done for he doesn't care, and only wishes himself somewhere else. The slightest movement of the ship cuts his breath like a blow. And he feels excited by the danger, too. The captain takes him aside. . . The life-boat can't come near us for more than an hour. Look here, Cloete, since you are here, and such a plucky one - do something for me. . . He tells him then that down in his cabin aft in a certain drawer there is a bundle of important papers and some sixty sovereigns in a small canvas bag. Asks Cloete to go and get these things out. He hasn't been below since the ship struck, and it seems to him that if he were to take his eyes off her she would fall to pieces. And then the men - a scared lot by this time - if he were to leave them by themselves they would attempt to launch one of the ship's boats in a panic at some heavier thump - and then some of them bound to get drowned. . . There are two or three boxes of matches about my shelves in my cabin if you want a light, says Captain Harry. Only wipe your wet hands before you begin to feel for them. . .

"Cloete doesn't like the job, but doesn't like to show funk, either - and he goes. Lots of water on the main-deck, and he splashes along; it was getting dark, too. All at once, by the mainmast, somebody catches him by the arm. Stafford. He wasn't thinking of Stafford at all. Captain Harry had said something as to the mate not being quite satisfactory, but it wasn't much. Cloete doesn't recognise him in his oilskins at first. He sees a white face with big eyes peering at him. . . Are you pleased, Mr. Cloete . . . ?

"Cloete is moved to laugh at the whine, and shakes him off. But the fellow scrambles on after him on the poop and follows him down into the cabin of that wrecked ship. And there they are, the two of them; can hardly see each other. . . You don't mean to make me believe you have had anything to do with this, says Cloete. . .

"They both shiver, nearly out of their wits with the excitement of being on board that ship. She thumps and lurches, and they stagger together, feeling sick. Cloete again bursts out laughing at that wretched creature Stafford pretending to have been up to something so desperate. . . Is that how you think you can treat me now? Yells the other man all of a sudden.

"A sea strikes the stern, the ship trembles and groans all round them, there's the noise of the seas about and overhead, confusing Cloete, and he hears the other screaming as if crazy. . . Ah, you don't believe me! Go and look at the port chain. Parted? Eh? Go and see if it's parted. Go and find the broken link. You can't. There's no broken link. That means a thousand pounds for me. No less. A thousand the day after we get ashore - prompt. I won't wait till she breaks up, Mr. Cloete. To the underwriters I go if I've to walk to London on my bare feet. Port cable! Look at her port cable, I will say to them. I doctored it - for the owners - tempted by a low rascal called Cloete.

"Cloete does not understand what it means exactly. All he sees is that the fellow means to make mischief. He sees trouble ahead. . .Do you think you can scare me? he asks, - you poor miserable skunk. . . And Stafford faces him out - both holding on to the cabin table: No, damn you , you are only a dirty vagabond; but I can scare the other, the chap in the black coat. . .

"Meaning George Dunbar. Cloete's brain reels at the thought. He doesn't imagine the fellow can do any real harm, but he knows what George is; give the show away; upset the whole business he had set his heart on. He says nothing; he hears the other, what with the funk and strain and excitement, panting like a dog - and then a snarl. . . A thousand down, twenty-four hours after we get ashore; day after to-morrow. That's my last word, Mr. Cloete. . . A thousand pounds, day after to-morrow, says Cloete. Oh yes. And to-day take this, you dirty cur. . . He hits straight from the shoulder in sheer rage, nothing else. Stafford goes away spinning along the bulk-head. Seeing this, Cloete steps out and lands him another one somewhere about the jaw. The fellow staggers backward right into the captain's cabin through the open door. Cloete, following him up, hears him fall down heavily and roll to leeward, then slams the door to and turns the key. . . There! says he to himself, that will stop you from making trouble."

"By Jove!" I murmured.

The old fellow departed from his impressive immobility to turn his rakishly hatted head and look at me with his old, black, lack-lustre eyes.

"He did leave him there," he uttered, weightily, returning to the contemplation of the wall. "Cloete didn't mean to allow anybody, let alone a thing like Stafford, to stand in the way of his great notion of making George and himself, and Captain Harry, too, for that matter, rich men. And he didn't think much of consequences. These patent-medicine chaps don't care what they say or what they do. They think the world's bound to swallow any story they like to tell. . . He stands listening for a bit. And it gives him quite a turn to hear a thump at the door and a sort of muffled raving screech inside the captain's room. He thinks he hears his own name, too, through the awful crash as the old Sagamore rises and falls to a sea. That noise and that awful shock make him clear out of the cabin. He collects his senses on the poop. But his heart sinks a little at the black wildness of the night. Chances that he will get drowned himself before long. Puts his head down the companion. Through the wind and breaking seas he can hear the noise of Stafford's beating against the door and cursing. He listens and says to himself: No. Can't trust him now. . .

"When he gets back to the top of the deck-house he says to Captain Harry, who asks him if he got the things, that he is very sorry. There was something wrong with the door. Couldn't open it. And to tell you the truth, says he, I didn't like to stop any longer in that cabin. There are noises there as if the ship were going to pieces. . . Captain Harry thinks: Nervous; can't be anything wrong with the door. But he says: Thanks - never mind, never mind. . . All hands looking out now for the life-boat. Everybody thinking of himself rather. Cloete asks himself, will they miss him? But the fact is that Mr. Stafford had made such poor show at sea that after the ship struck nobody ever paid any attention to him. Nobody cared what he did or where he was. Pitch dark, too - no counting of heads. The light of the tug with the lifeboat in tow is seen making for the ship, and Captain Harry asks: Are we all there? . . . Somebody answers: All here, sir. . . Stand by to leave the ship, then, says Captain Harry; and two of you help the gentleman over first. . . Aye, aye, sir. . . Cloete was moved to ask Captain Harry to let him stay till last, but the life-boat drops on a grapnel abreast the fore-rigging, two chaps lay hold of him, watch their chance, and drop him into her, all safe.

"He's nearly exhausted; not used to that sort of thing, you see. He sits in the stern-sheets with his eyes shut. Don't want to look at the white water boiling all around. The men drop into the boat one after another. Then he hears Captain Harry's voice shouting in the wind to the coxswain, to hold on a moment, and some other words he can't catch, and the coxswain yelling back: Don't be long, sir. . . What is it? Cloete asks feeling faint. . . Something about the ship's papers, says the coxswain, very anxious. It's no time to be fooling about alongside, you understand. They haul the boat off a little and wait. The water flies over her in sheets. Cloete's senses almost leave him. He thinks of nothing. He's numb all over, till there's a shout: Here he is! . . . They see a figure in the fore-rigging waiting - they slack away on the grapnel-line and get him in the boat quite easy. There is a little shouting - it's all mixed up with the noise of the sea. Cloete fancies that Stafford's voice is talking away quite close to his ear. There's a lull in the wind, and Stafford's voice seems to be speaking very fast to the coxswain; he tells him that of course he was near his skipper, was all the time near him, till the old man said at the last moment that he must go and get the ship's papers from aft; would insist on going himself; told him, Stafford, to get into the life-boat. . . He had meant to wait for his skipper, only there came this smooth of the seas, and he thought he would take his chance at once.

"Cloete opens his eyes. Yes. There's Stafford sitting close by him in that crowded life-boat. The coxswain stoops over Cloete and cries: Did you hear what the mate said, sir? . . . Cloete's face feels as if it were set in plaster, lips and all. Yes, I did, he forces himself to answer. The coxswain waits a moment, then says: I don't like it. . . And he turns to the mate, telling him it was a pity he did not try to run along the deck and hurry up the captain when the lull came. Stafford answers at once that he did think of it, only he was afraid of missing him on the deck in the dark. For, says he, the captain might have got over at once, thinking I was already in the life-boat, and you would have hauled off perhaps, leaving me behind. . . True enough, says the coxswain. A minute or so passes. This won't do, mutters the coxswain. Suddenly Stafford speaks up in a sort of hollow voice: I was by when he told Mr. Cloete here that he didn't know how he would ever have the courage to leave the old ship; didn't he, now? And Cloete feels his arm being gripped quietly in the dark. . . Didn't he now? We were standing together just before you went over, Mr. Cloete? . . .

"Just then the coxswain cries out: I'm going on board to see. . . Cloete tears his arm away: I am going with you. . .

"When they get aboard, the coxswain tells Cloete to go aft along one side of the ship and he would go along the other so as not to miss the captain. . . And feel about with your hands, too, says he; he might have fallen and be lying insensible somewhere on the deck. When Cloete gets at last to the cabin companion on the poop the coxswain is already there, peering down and sniffing. I detect a smell of smoke down there, says he. And he yells: Are you there, sir? . . . This is not a case for shouting, says Cloete, feeling his heart go stony, as it were. . . Down they go. Pitch dark; the inclination so sharp that the coxswain, groping his way into the captain's room, slips and goes tumbling down. Cloete hears him cry out as though he had hurt himself, and asks what's the matter. And the coxswain answers quietly that he had fallen on the captain, lying there insensible. Cloete without a word begins to grope all over the shelves for a box of matches, finds one, and strikes a light. He sees the coxswain in his cork jacket kneeling over Captain Harry. . . Blood, says the coxswain, looking up, and the match goes out. . .

"Wait a bit, says Cloete; I'll make paper spills. . . He had felt the back of books on the shelves. And so he stands lighting one spill from another while the coxswain turns poor Captain Harry over. Dead, he says. Shot through the heart. Here's the revolver. . . He hands it up to Cloete, who looks at it before putting it in his pocket, and sees a plate on the butt with H. Dunbar on it. . . His own, he mutters. . . Whose else revolver did you expect to find? snaps the coxswain. And look, he took off his long oilskin in the cabin before he went in. But what's this lot of burnt paper? What could he want to burn the ship's papers for?

Cloete sees all, the little drawers drawn out, and asks the coxswain to look well into them. . . There's nothing, says the man. Cleaned out. Seems to have pulled out all he could lay his hands on and set fire to the lot. Mad - that's what it is - went mad. And now he's dead. You'll have to break it to his wife. . .

"I feel as if I were going mad myself, says Cloete, suddenly, and the coxswain begs him for God's sake to pull himself together, and drags him away from the cabin. They had to leave the body, and as it was they were just in time before a furious squall came on. Cloete is dragged into the life-boat and the coxswain tumbles in. Haul away on the grapnel, he shouts; the captain has shot himself.

"Cloete was like a dead man - didn't care for anything. He let that Stafford pinch his arm twice without making a sign. Most of Westport was on the old pier to see the men out of the life-boat, and at first there was a sort of confused cheery uproar when she came alongside; but after the coxswain has shouted something the voices die out, and everybody is very quiet. As soon as Cloete has set foot on something firm he becomes himself again. The coxswain shakes hands with him: Poor woman, poor woman, I'd rather you had the job than I. . .

"Where's the mate?" asks Cloete. He's the last man who spoke to the master. . . Somebody ran along - the crew were being taken to the Mission Hall, where there was a fire and shake-downs ready for them - somebody ran along the pier and caught up with Stafford. . .Here! The owner's agent wants you. . . Cloete tucks the fellow's arm under his own and walks away with him to the left, where the fishing-harbour is. . . I suppose I haven't misunderstood you. You wish me to look after you a bit, says he. The other hangs on him rather limp, but gives a nasty little laugh: You had better, he mumbles; but mind, no tricks; no tricks, Mr. Cloete; we are on land now.

"There's a police office within fifty yards from here, says Cloete. He turns into a little public house, pushes Stafford along the passage. The landlord runs out of the bar. . . This is the mate of the ship on the rocks, Cloete explains; I wish you would take care of him a bit to-night. . . What's the matter with him? asks the man. Stafford leans against the wall in the passage, looking ghastly. And Cloete says it's nothing - done up, of course. . . I will be responsible for the expense; I am the owner's agent. I'll be round in an hour or two to see him.

And Cloete gets back to the hotel. The news had travelled there already, and the first thing he sees is George outside the door as white as a sheet waiting for him. Cloete just gives him a nod and they go in. Mrs. Harry stands at the head of the stairs, and, when she sees only these two coming up, flings her arms above her head and runs into her room. Nobody had dared tell her, but not seeing her husband was enough. Cloete hears an awful shriek. . . Go to her, he says to George.

"While he's alone in the private parlour Cloete drinks a glass of brandy and thinks it all out. Then George comes in. . . The landlady's with her, he says. And he begins to walk up and down the room, flinging his arms about and talking, disconnected like, his face set hard as Cloete has never seen it before. . . What must be, must be. Dead - only brother. Well, dead - his troubles over. But we are living, he says to Cloete; and I suppose, says he, glaring at him with hot, dry eyes, that you won't forget to wire in the morning to your friend that we are coming in for certain. . .

"Meaning the patent-medicine fellow. . . Death is death and business is business, George goes on; and look - my hands are clean, he says, showing them to Cloete. Cloete thinks: He's going crazy. He catches hold of him by the shoulders and begins to shake him: Damn you - if you had had the sense to know what to say to your brother, if you had had the spunk to speak to him at all, you moral creature you, he would be alive now, he shouts.

"At this George stares, then bursts out weeping with a great bellow. He throws himself on the couch, buries his face in a cushion, and howls like a kid. . . That's better, thinks Cloete, and he leaves him, telling the landlord that he must go out, as he has some little business to attend to that night. The landlord's wife, weeping herself, catches him on the stairs: Oh, sir, that poor lady will go out of her mind. . .

"Cloete shakes her off, thinking to himself: Oh no! She won't. She will get over it. Nobody will go mad about this affair unless I do. It isn't sorrow that makes people go mad, but worry.

"There Cloete was wrong. What affected Mrs. Harry was that her husband should take his own life, with her, as it were, looking on. She brooded over it so that in less than a year they had to put her into a Home. She was very, very quiet; just gentle melancholy. She lived for quite a long time.

"Well, Cloete splashes along in the wind and rain. Nobody in the streets - all the excitement over. The publican runs out to meet him in the passage and says to him: Not this way. He isn't in his room. We couldn't get him to go to bed nohow. He's in the little parlour there. We've lighted him a fire. . . You have been giving him drinks too, says Cloete; I never said I would be responsible for drinks. How many? . . . Two, says the other. It's all right. I don't mind doing that much for a shipwrecked sailor. . . Cloete smiles his funny smile: Eh? Come. He paid for them. . . The publican just blinks. . . Gave you gold, didn't he? Speak up! . . . What of that! cries the man. What are you after, anyway? He had the right change for his sovereign.

"Just so, says Cloete. He walks into the parlour, and there he sees our Stafford; hair all up on end, landlord's shirt and pants on, bare feet in slippers, sitting by the fire. When he sees Cloete he casts his eyes down.

"You didn't mean us ever to meet again, Mr. Cloete, Stafford says, demurely. . . That fellow, when he had the drink he wanted - he wasn't a drunkard - would put on this sort of sly, modest air. . . But since the captain committed suicide, he says, I have been sitting here thinking it out. All sorts of things happen. Conspiracy to lose the ship - attempted murder - and this suicide. For if it was not suicide, Mr. Cloete, then I know of a victim of the most cruel, cold-blooded attempt at murder; somebody who has suffered a thousand deaths. And that makes the thousand pounds of which we spoke once a quite insignificant sum. Look how very convenient this suicide is. . .

"He looks up at Cloete then, who smiles at him and comes quite close to the table.

"You killed Harry Dunbar, he whispers. . . The fellow glares at him and shows his teeth: Of course I did! I had been in that cabin for an hour and a half like a rat in a trap. . . Shut up and left to drown in that wreck. Let flesh and blood judge. Of course I shot him! I thought it was you, you murdering scoundrel, come back to settle me. He opens the door flying and tumbles right down upon me; I had a revolver in my hand, and I shot him. I was crazy. Men have gone crazy for less.

"Cloete looks at him without flinching. Aha! That's your story, is it? . . . And he shakes the table a little in his passion as he speaks. . . Now listen to mine. What's this conspiracy? Who's going to prove it? You were there to rob. You were rifling his cabin; he came upon you unawares with your hands in the drawer; and you shot him with his own revolver. You killed to steal - to steal! His brother and the clerks in the office know that he took sixty pounds with him to sea. Sixty pounds in gold in a canvas bag. He told me where they were. The coxswain of the life-boat can swear to it that the drawers were all empty. And you are such a fool that before you're half an hour ashore you change a sovereign to pay for a drink. Listen to me. If you don't turn up day after to-morrow at George Dunbar's solicitors, to make the proper deposition as to the loss of the ship, I shall set the police on your track. Day after to-morrow. . .

"And then what do you think? That Stafford begins to tear his hair. Just so. Tugs at it with both hands without saying anything. Cloete gives a push to the table which nearly sends the fellow off his chair, tumbling inside the fender; so that he has got to catch hold of it to save himself. . .

"You know the sort of man I am, Cloete says, fiercely. I've got to a point that I don't care what happens to me. I would shoot you now for tuppence.

"At this the cur dodges under the table. Then Cloete goes out, and as he turns in the street - you know, little fishermen's cottages, all dark; raining in torrents, too - the other opens the window of the parlour and speaks in a sort of crying voice -

"You low Yankee fiend - I'll pay you off some day.

"Cloete passes by with a damn bitter laugh, because he

thinks that the fellow in a way has paid him off already, if he only knew it."

My impressive ruffian drank what remained of his beer, while his black, sunken eyes looked at me over the rim.

"I don't quite understand this," I said. "In what way?"

He unbent a little and explained without too much scorn that Captain Harry being dead, his half of the insurance money went to his wife, and her trustees of course bought consols with it. Enough to keep her comfortable. George Dunbar's half, as Cloete feared from the first, did not prove sufficient to launch the medicine well; other moneyed men stepped in, and these two had to go out of that business, pretty nearly shorn of everything.

"I am curious," I said, "to learn what the motive force of this tragic affair was - I mean the patent medicine. Do you know?"

He named it, and I whistled respectfully. Nothing less than Parker's Lively Lumbago Pills. Enormous property! You know it; all the world knows it. Every second man, at least, on this globe of ours has tried it.

"Why!" I cried, "they missed an immense fortune."

"Yes," he mumbled, "by the price of a revolver-shot."

He told me also that eventually Cloete returned to the States, passenger in a cargo-boat from Albert Dock. The night before he sailed he met him wandering about the quays, and took him home for a drink. "Funny chap, Cloete. We sat all night drinking grogs, till it was time for him to go on board."

It was then that Cloete, unembittered but weary, told him this story, with that utterly unconscious frankness of a patent-medicine man stranger to all moral standards. Cloete concluded by remarking that he, had "had enough of the old country." George Dunbar had turned on him, too, in the end. Cloete was clearly somewhat disillusioned.

As to Stafford, he died, professed loafer, in some East End hospital or other, and on his last day clamoured "for a parson," because his conscience worried him for killing an innocent man. "Wanted somebody to tell him it was all right," growled my old ruffian, contemptuously. "He told the parson that I knew this Cloete who had tried to murder him, and so the parson (he worked among the dock labourers) once spoke to me about it. That skunk of a fellow finding himself trapped yelled for mercy. . . Promised to be good and so on. . . Then he went crazy . . . screamed and threw himself about, beat his head against the bulkheads . . . you can guess all that - eh? . . . till he was exhausted. Gave up. Threw himself down, shut his eyes, and wanted to pray. So he says. Tried to think of some prayer for a quick death - he was that terrified. Thought that if he had a knife or something he would cut his throat, and be done with it. Then he thinks: No! Would try to cut away the wood about the lock. . . He had no knife in his pocket. . . he was weeping and calling on God to send him a tool of some kind when suddenly he thinks: Axe! In most ships there is a spare emergency axe kept in the master's room in some locker or other. . . Up he jumps. . . Pitch dark. "Pulls at the drawers to find matches and, groping for them, the first thing he comes upon - Captain Harry's revolver. Loaded too. He goes perfectly quiet all over. Can shoot the lock to pieces. See? Saved! God's providence! There are boxes of matches too. Thinks he: I may just as well see what I am about.

"Strikes a light and sees the little canvas bag tucked away at the back of the drawer. Knew at once what that was. Rams it into his pocket quick. Aha! says he to himself: this requires more light. So he pitches a lot of paper on the floor, set fire to it, and starts in a hurry rummaging for more valuables. Did you ever? He told that East-End parson that the devil tempted him. First God's mercy - then devil's work. Turn and turn about.

"Any squirming skunk can talk like that. He was so busy with the drawers that the first thing he heard was a shout, Great Heavens. He looks up and there was the door open (Cloete had left the key in the lock) and Captain Harry holding on, well above him, very fierce in the light of the burning papers. His eyes were starting out of his head. Thieving, he thunders at him. A sailor! An officer! No! A wretch like you deserves no better than to be left here to drown.

"This Stafford - on his death-bed - told the parson that when he heard these words he went crazy again. He snatched his hand with the revolver in it out of the drawer, and fired without aiming. Captain Harry fell right in with a crash like a stone on top of the burning papers, putting the blaze out. All dark. Not a sound. He listened for a bit then dropped the revolver and scrambled out on deck like mad."

The old fellow struck the table with his ponderous fist.

"What makes me sick is to hear these silly boat-men telling people the captain committed suicide. Pah! Captain Harry was a man that could face his Maker any time up there, and here below, too. He wasn't the sort to slink out of life. Not he! He was a good man down to the ground. He gave me my first job as stevedore only three days after I got married."

As the vindication of Captain Harry from the charge of suicide seemed to be his only object, I did not thank him very effusively for his material. And then it was not worth many thanks in any case.

For it is too startling even to think of such things happening in our respectable Channel in full view, so to speak, of the luxurious continental traffic to Switzerland and Monte Carlo. This story to be acceptable should have been transposed to somewhere in the South Seas. But it would have been too much trouble to cook it for the consumption of magazine readers. So here it is raw, so to speak - just as it was told to me - but unfortunately robbed of the striking effect of the narrator; the most imposing old ruffian that ever followed the unromantic trade of master stevedore in the port of London.

Oct. 1910.

THE INN OF THE TWO WITCHES - A FIND

This tale, episode, experience - call it how you will -
was related in the fifties of the last century by a man
who, by his own confession, was sixty years old at the
time. Sixty is not a bad age - unless in perspective,
when no doubt it is contemplated by the majority of us
with mixed feelings. It is a calm age; the game is
practically over by then; and standing aside one begins
to remember with a certain vividness what a fine
fellow one used to be. I have observed that, by an
amiable attention of Providence, most people at sixty
begin to take a romantic view of themselves. Their
very failures exhale a charm of peculiar potency. And
indeed the hopes of the future are a fine company to
live with, exquisite forms, fascinating if you like, but -
so to speak - naked, stripped for a run. The robes of
glamour are luckily the property of the immovable past
which, without them, would sit, a shivery sort of thing,
under the gathering shadows.

I suppose it was the romanticism of growing age which
set our man to relate his experience for his own
satisfaction or for the wonder of his posterity. It could
not have been for his glory, because the experience
was simply that of an abominable fright - terror he
calls it. You would have guessed that the relation
alluded to in the very first lines was in writing.

This writing constitutes the Find declared in the sub-title. The title itself is my own contrivance, (can't call it invention), and has the merit of veracity. We will be concerned with an inn here. As to the witches that's merely a conventional expression, and we must take our man's word for it that it fits the case.

The Find was made in a box of books bought in London, in a street which no longer exists, from a second-hand bookseller in the last stage of decay. As to the books themselves they were at least twentieth-hand, and on inspection turned out not worth the very small sum of money I disbursed. It might have been some premonition of that fact which made me say: "But I must have the box too." The decayed bookseller assented by the careless, tragic gesture of a man already doomed to extinction.

A litter of loose pages at the bottom of the box excited my curiosity but faintly. The close, neat, regular handwriting was not attractive at first sight. But in one place the statement that in A.D. 1813 the writer was twenty-two years old caught my eye. Two and twenty is an interesting age in which one is easily reckless and easily frightened; the faculty of reflection being weak and the power of imagination strong.

In another place the phrase: "At night we stood in again," arrested my languid attention, because it was a sea phrase. "Let's see what it is all about," I thought, without excitement.

Oh! but it was a dull-faced MS., each line resembling every other line in their close-set and regular order. It was like the drone of a monotonous voice. A treatise on sugar-refining (the dreariest subject I can think of) could have been given a more lively appearance. "In A.D. 1813, I was twenty-two years old," he begins earnestly and goes on with every appearance of calm, horrible industry. Don't imagine, however, that there is anything archaic in my find. Diabolic ingenuity in invention though as old as the world is by no means a lost art. Look at the telephones for shattering the little peace of mind given to us in this world, or at the machine guns for letting with dispatch life out of our bodies. Now-a-days any blear-eyed old witch if only strong enough to turn an insignificant little handle could lay low a hundred young men of twenty in the twinkling of an eye.

If this isn't progress! . . . Why immense! We have moved on, and so you must expect to meet here a certain naiveness of contrivance and simplicity of aim appertaining to the remote epoch. And of course no motoring tourist can hope to find such an inn anywhere, now. This one, the one of the title, was situated in Spain. That much I discovered only from internal evidence, because a good many pages of that relation were missing - perhaps not a great misfortune after all. The writer seemed to have entered into a most elaborate detail of the why and wherefore of his presence on that coast - presumably the north coast of Spain. His experience has nothing to do with the sea, though. As far as I can make it out, he was an officer on board a sloop-of-war. There's nothing strange in that. At all stages of the long Peninsular campaign many of our men-of-war of the smaller kind were cruising off the north coast of Spain-as risky and disagreeable a station as can be well imagined.

It looks as though that ship of his had had some special service to perform. A careful explanation of all the circumstances was to be expected from our man, only, as I've said, some of his pages (good tough paper too) were missing: gone in covers for jampots or in wadding for the fowling-pieces of his irreverent posterity. But it is to be seen clearly that communication with the shore and even the sending of messengers inland was part of her service, either to obtain intelligence from or to transmit orders or advice to patriotic Spaniards, guerilleros or secret juntas of the province. Something of the sort. All this can be only inferred from the preserved scraps of his conscientious writing.

Next we come upon the panegyric of a very fine sailor, a member of the ship's company, having the rating of the captain's coxswain. He was known on board as Cuba Tom; not because he was Cuban however; he was indeed the best type of a genuine British tar of that time, and a man-of-war's man for years. He came by the name on account of some wonderful adventures he had in that island in his young days, adventures which were the favourite subject of the yarns he was in the habit of spinning to his shipmates of an evening on the forecastle head. He was intelligent, very strong, and of proved courage. Incidentally we are told, so exact is our narrator, that Tom had the finest pigtail for thickness and length of any man in the Navy. This appendage, much cared for and sheathed tightly in a porpoise skin, hung half way down his broad back to the great admiration of all beholders and to the great envy of some.

Our young officer dwells on the manly qualities of Cuba Tom with something like affection. This sort of relation between officer and man was not then very rare. A youngster on joining the service was put under the charge of a trustworthy seaman, who slung his first hammock for him and often later on became a sort of humble friend to the junior officer. The narrator on joining the sloop had found this man on board after some years of separation. There is something touching in the warm pleasure he remembers and records at this meeting with the professional mentor of his boyhood.

We discover then that, no Spaniard being forthcoming for the service, this worthy seaman with the unique pigtail and a very high character for courage and steadiness had been selected as messenger for one of these missions inland which have been mentioned. His preparations were not elaborate. One gloomy autumn morning the sloop ran close to a shallow cove where a landing could be made on that iron-bound shore. A boat was lowered, and pulled in with Tom Corbin (Cuba Tom) perched in the bow, and our young man (Mr. Edgar Byrne was his name on this earth which knows him no more) sitting in the stern sheets.

A few inhabitants of a hamlet, whose grey stone houses could be seen a hundred yards or so up a deep ravine, had come down to the shore and watched the approach of the boat. The two Englishmen leaped ashore. Either from dullness or astonishment the peasants gave no greeting, and only fell back in silence.

Mr. Byrne had made up his mind to see Tom Corbin started fairly on his way. He looked round at the heavy surprised faces.

"There isn't much to get out of them," he said. "Let us walk up to the village. There will be a wine shop for sure where we may find somebody more promising to talk to and get some information from."

"Aye, aye, sir," said Tom falling into step behind his officer. "A bit of palaver as to courses and distances can do no harm; I crossed the broadest part of Cuba by the help of my tongue tho' knowing far less Spanish than I do now. As they say themselves it was 'four words and no more' with me, that time when I got left behind on shore by the Blanche, frigate."

He made light of what was before him, which was but a day's journey into the mountains. It is true that there was a full day's journey before striking the mountain path, but that was nothing for a man who had crossed the island of Cuba on his two legs, and with no more than four words of the language to begin with.

The officer and the man were walking now on a thick sodden bed of dead leaves, which the peasants thereabouts accumulate in the streets of their villages to rot during the winter for field manure. Turning his head Mr. Byrne perceived that the whole male population of the hamlet was following them on the noiseless springy carpet. Women stared from the doors of the houses and the children had apparently gone into hiding. The village knew the ship by sight, afar off, but no stranger had landed on that spot perhaps for a hundred years or more. The cocked hat of Mr. Byrne, the bushy whiskers and the enormous pigtail of the sailor, filled them with mute wonder. They pressed behind the two Englishmen staring like those islanders discovered by Captain Cook in the South Seas.

It was then that Byrne had his first glimpse of the little cloaked man in a yellow hat. Faded and dingy as it was, this covering for his head made him noticeable.

The entrance to the wine shop was like a rough hole in a wall of flints. The owner was the only person who was not in the street, for he came out from the darkness at the back where the inflated forms of wine skins hung on nails could be vaguely distinguished. He was a tall, one-eyed Asturian with scrubby, hollow cheeks; a grave expression of countenance contrasted enigmatically with the roaming restlessness of his solitary eye. On learning that the matter in hand was the sending on his way of that English mariner toward a certain Gonzales in the mountains, he closed his good eye for a moment as if in meditation. Then opened it, very lively again.

"Possibly, possibly. It could be done."

A friendly murmur arose in the group in the doorway at the name of Gonzales, the local leader against the French. Inquiring as to the safety of the road Byrne was glad to learn that no troops of that nation had been seen in the neighbourhood for months. Not the smallest little detachment of these impious polizones. While giving these answers the owner of the wine-shop busied himself in drawing into an earthenware jug some wine which he set before the heretic English, pocketing with grave abstraction the small piece of money the officer threw upon the table in recognition of the unwritten law that none may enter a wine-shop without buying drink. His eye was in constant motion as if it were trying to do the work of the two; but when Byrne made inquiries as to the possibility of hiring a mule, it became immovably fixed in the direction of the door which was closely besieged by the curious. In front of them, just within the threshold, the little man in the large cloak and yellow hat had taken his stand. He was a diminutive person, a mere homunculus,

Byrne describes him, in a ridiculously mysterious, yet assertive attitude, a corner of his cloak thrown cavalierly over his left shoulder, muffling his chin and mouth; while the broad-brimmed yellow hat hung on a corner of his square little head. He stood there taking snuff, repeatedly.

"A mule," repeated the wine-seller, his eyes fixed on that quaint and snuffy figure. . . "No, senor officer! Decidedly no mule is to be got in this poor place."

The coxswain , who stood by with the true sailor's air of unconcern in strange surroundings, struck in quietly -

"If your honour will believe me Shank's pony's the best for this job. I would have to leave the beast somewhere, anyhow, since the captain has told me that half my way will be along paths fit only for goats."

The diminutive man made a step forward, and speaking through the folds of the cloak which seemed to muffle a sarcastic intention -

"Si, senor. They are too honest in this village to have a single mule amongst them for your worship's service. To that I can bear testimony. In these times it's only rogues or very clever men who can manage to have mules or any other four-footed beasts and the wherewithal to keep them. But what this valiant mariner wants is a guide; and here, senor, behold my brother-in-law, Bernardino, wine-seller, and alcade of this most Christian and hospitable village, who will find you one."

This, Mr. Byrne says in his relation, was the only thing

to do. A youth in a ragged coat and goat-skin breeches was produced after some more talk. The English officer stood treat to the whole village, and while the peasants drank he and Cuba Tom took their departure accompanied by the guide. The diminutive man in the cloak had disappeared.

Byrne went along with the coxswain out of the village. He wanted to see him fairly on his way; and he would have gone a greater distance, if the seaman had not suggested respectfully the advisability of return so as not to keep the ship a moment longer than necessary so close in with the shore on such an unpromising looking morning. A wild gloomy sky hung over their heads when they took leave of each other, and their surroundings of rank bushes and stony fields were dreary.

"In four days' time," were Byrne's last words, "the ship will stand in and send a boat on shore if the weather permits. If not you'll have to make it out on shore the best you can till we come along to take you off."

"Right you are, sir," answered Tom, and strode on. Byrne watched him step out on a narrow path. In a thick pea-jacket with a pair of pistols in his belt, a cutlass by his side, and a stout cudgel in his hand, he looked a sturdy figure and well able to take care of himself. He turned round for a moment to wave his hand, giving to Byrne one more view of his honest bronzed face with bushy whiskers. The lad in goatskin breeches looking, Byrne says, like a faun or a young satyr leaping ahead, stopped to wait for him, and then went off at a bound. Both disappeared.

Byrne turned back. The hamlet was hidden in a fold of the ground, and the spot seemed the most lonely corner of the earth and as if accursed in its uninhabited desolate barrenness. Before he had walked many yards, there appeared very suddenly from behind a bush the muffled up diminutive Spaniard. Naturally Byrne stopped short.

The other made a mysterious gesture with a tiny hand peeping from under his cloak. His hat hung very much at the side of his head. "Senor," he said without any preliminaries. "Caution! It is a positive fact that one-eyed Bernardino, my brother-in-law, has at this moment a mule in his stable. And why he who is not clever has a mule there? Because he is a rogue; a man without conscience. Because I had to give up the macho to him to secure for myself a roof to sleep under and a mouthful of olla to keep my soul in this insignificant body of mine. Yet, senor, it contains a heart many times bigger than the mean thing which beats in the breast of that brute connection of mine of which I am ashamed, though I opposed that marriage with all my power. Well, the misguided woman suffered enough. She had her purgatory on this earth - God rest her soul."

Byrne says he was so astonished by the sudden appearance of that sprite-like being, and by the sardonic bitterness of the speech, that he was unable to disentangle the significant fact from what seemed but a piece of family history fired out at him without rhyme or reason. Not at first. He was confounded and at the same time he was impressed by the rapid forcible delivery, quite different from the frothy excited loquacity of an Italian. So he stared while the homunculus letting his cloak fall about him, aspired an immense quantity of snuff out of the hollow of his palm.

" A mule , " exclaimed Byrne seizing at last the real aspect of the discourse. "You say he has got a mule? That's queer! Why did he refuse to let me have it?"

The diminutive Spaniard muffled himself up again with great dignity.

"Quien sabe," he said coldly, with a shrug of his draped shoulders. "He is a great politico in everything he does. But one thing your worship may be certain of - that his intentions are always rascally. This husband of my defunta sister ought to have been married a long time ago to the widow with the wooden legs." {1}

"I see. But remember that; whatever your motives, your worship countenanced him in this lie."

The bright unhappy eyes on each side of a predatory nose confronted Byrne without wincing, while with that testiness which lurks so often at the bottom of Spanish dignity -

"No doubt the senor officer would not lose an ounce of blood if I were stuck under the fifth rib," he retorted. "But what of this poor sinner here?" Then changing his tone. "Senor, by the necessities of the times I live here in exile, a Castilian and an old Christian, existing miserably in the midst of these brute Asturians, and dependent on the worst of them all, who has less conscience and scruples than a wolf. And being a man of intelligence I govern myself accordingly. Yet I can hardly contain my scorn. You have heard the way I spoke. A caballero of parts like your worship might have guessed that there was a cat in there."

" What cat ? " said Byrne uneasily. " Oh , I see. Something suspicious. No, senor. I guessed nothing. My nation are not good guessers at that sort of thing; and, therefore, I ask you plainly whether that wine-seller has spoken the truth in other particulars?"

"There are certainly no Frenchmen anywhere about," said the little man with a return to his indifferent manner.

"Or robbers - ladrones?"

"Ladrones en grande - no! Assuredly not," was the answer in a cold philosophical tone. "What is there left for them to do after the French? And nobody travels in these times. But who can say! Opportunity makes the robber. Still that mariner of yours has a fierce aspect, and with the son of a cat rats will have no play. But there is a saying, too, that where honey is there will soon be flies."

This oracular discourse exasperated Byrne. "In the name of God," he cried, "tell me plainly if you think my man is reasonably safe on his journey."

The homunculus, undergoing one of his rapid changes, seized the officer's arm. The grip of his little hand was astonishing.

"Senor! Bernardino had taken notice of him. What more do you want? And listen - men have disappeared on this road - on a certain portion of this road, when Bernardino kept a meson, an inn, and I, his brother-in-law, had coaches and mules for hire. Now there are no travellers, no coaches. The French have ruined me. Bernardino has retired here for reasons of his own after my sister died. They were three to torment the life out of her, he and Erminia and Lucilla, two aunts of his - all affiliated to the devil. And now he has robbed me of my last mule. You are an armed man. Demand the macho from him, with a pistol to his head, senor - it is not his, I tell you - and ride after your man who is so precious to you. And then you shall both be safe, for no two travellers have been ever known to disappear together in those days. As to the beast, I, its owner, I confide it to your honour."

They were staring hard at each other, and Byrne nearly burst into a laugh at the ingenuity and transparency of the little man's plot to regain possession of his mule. But he had no difficulty to keep a straight face because he felt deep within himself a strange inclination to do that very extraordinary thing. He did not laugh, but his lip quivered; at which the diminutive Spaniard, detaching his black glittering eyes from Byrne's face, turned his back on him brusquely with a gesture and a fling of the cloak which somehow expressed contempt, bitterness, and discouragement all at once. He turned away and stood still, his hat aslant, muffled up to the ears. But he was not offended to the point of refusing the silver duro which Byrne offered him with a non-committal speech as if nothing extraordinary had passed between them.

"I must make haste on board now," said Byrne, then.

"Vaya usted con Dios," muttered the gnome. And this interview ended with a sarcastic low sweep of the hat which was replaced at the same perilous angle as before.

Directly the boat had been hoisted the ship's sails were

filled on the off-shore tack, and Byrne imparted the whole story to his captain, who was but a very few years older than himself. There was some amused indignation at it - but while they laughed they looked gravely at each other. A Spanish dwarf trying to beguile an officer of his majesty's navy into stealing a mule for him - that was too funny, too ridiculous, too incredible. Those were the exclamations of the captain. He couldn't get over the grotesqueness of it.

"Incredible. That's just it," murmured Byrne at last in a significant tone.

They exchanged a long stare. "It's as clear as daylight," affirmed the captain impatiently, because in his heart he was not certain. And Tom the best seaman in the ship for one, the good-humouredly deferential friend of his boyhood for the other, was becoming endowed with a compelling fascination, like a symbolic figure of loyalty appealing to their feelings and their conscience, so that they could not detach their thoughts from his safety. Several times they went up on deck, only to look at the coast, as if it could tell them something of his fate. It stretched away, lengthening in the distance, mute, naked, and savage, veiled now and then by the slanting cold shafts of rain. The westerly swell rolled its interminable angry lines of foam and big dark clouds flew over the ship in a sinister procession.

"I wish to goodness you had done what your little friend in the yellow hat wanted you to do," said the commander of the sloop late in the afternoon with visible exasperation.

"Do you, sir?" answered Byrne, bitter with positive anguish. "I wonder what you would have said afterwards? Why! I might have been kicked out of the service for looting a mule from a nation in alliance with His Majesty. Or I might have been battered to a pulp with flails and pitch-forks - a pretty tale to get abroad about one of your officers - while trying to steal a mule. Or chased ignominiously to the boat - for you would not have expected me to shoot down unoffending people for the sake of a mangy mule. . . And yet," he added in a low voice, "I almost wish myself I had done it."

Before dark those two young men had worked themselves up into a highly complex psychological state of scornful scepticism and alarmed credulity. It tormented them exceedingly; and the thought that it would have to last for six days at least, and possibly be prolonged further for an indefinite time, was not to be borne. The ship was therefore put on the inshore tack at dark. All through the gusty dark night she went towards the land to look for her man, at times lying over in the heavy puffs, at others rolling idle in the swell, nearly stationary, as if she too had a mind of her own to swing perplexed between cool reason and warm impulse.

Then just at daybreak a boat put off from her and went on tossed by the seas towards the shallow cove where, with considerable difficulty, an officer in a thick coat and a round hat managed to land on a strip of shingle.

"It was my wish," writes Mr. Byrne, "a wish of which my captain approved, to land secretly if possible. I did not want to be seen either by my aggrieved friend in the yellow hat, whose motives were not clear, or by the one-eyed wine-seller, who may or may not have been affiliated to the devil, or indeed by any other dweller in that primitive village. But unfortunately the cove was the only possible landing place for miles; and from the steepness of the ravine I couldn't make a circuit to avoid the houses."

"Fortunately," he goes on, "all the people were yet in their beds. It was barely daylight when I found myself walking on the thick layer of sodden leaves filling the only street. No soul was stirring abroad, no dog barked. The silence was profound, and I had concluded with some wonder that apparently no dogs were kept in the hamlet, when I heard a low snarl, and from a noisome alley between two hovels emerged a vile cur with its tail between its legs. He slunk off silently showing me his teeth as he ran before me, and he disappeared so suddenly that he might have been the unclean incarnation of the Evil One. There was, too, something so weird in the manner of its coming and vanishing, that my spirits, already by no means very high, became further depressed by the revolting sight of this creature as if by an unlucky presage."

He got away from the coast unobserved, as far as he knew, then struggled manfully to the west against wind and rain, on a barren dark upland, under a sky of ashes. Far away the harsh and desolate mountains raising their scarped and denuded ridges seemed to wait for him menacingly. The evening found him fairly near to them, but, in sailor language, uncertain of his position, hungry, wet, and tired out by a day of steady tramping over broken ground during which he had seen very few people, and had been unable to obtain the slightest intelligence of Tom Corbin's passage. "On! on! I must push on," he had been saying to himself through the hours of solitary effort, spurred more by incertitude than by any definite fear or definite hope.

The lowering daylight died out quickly, leaving him faced by a broken bridge. He descended into the ravine, forded a narrow stream by the last gleam of rapid water, and clambering out on the other side was met by the night which fen like a bandage over his eyes. The wind sweeping in the darkness the broadside of the sierra worried his ears by a continuous roaring noise as of a maddened sea. He suspected that he had lost the road. Even in daylight, with its ruts and mud-holes and ledges of outcropping stone, it was difficult to distinguish from the dreary waste of the moor interspersed with boulders and clumps of naked bushes. But, as he says, "he steered his course by the feel of the wind," his hat rammed low on his brow, his head down, stopping now and again from mere weariness of mind rather than of body - as if not his strength but his resolution were being overtaxed by the strain of endeavour half suspected to be vain, and by the unrest of his feelings.

In one of these pauses borne in the wind faintly as if from very far away he heard a sound of knocking, just knocking on wood. He noticed that the wind had lulled suddenly.

His heart started beating tumultuously because in himself he carried the impression of the desert solitudes he had been traversing for the last six hours - the oppressive sense of an uninhabited world. When he raised his head a gleam of light, illusory as it often happens in dense darkness, swam before his eyes. While he peered, the sound of feeble knocking was repeated - and suddenly he felt rather than saw the existence of a massive obstacle in his path. What was it? The spur of a hill? Or was it a house! Yes. It was a house right close, as though it had risen from the ground or had come gliding to meet him, dumb and pallid; from some dark recess of the night. It towered loftily. He had come up under its lee; another three steps and he could have touched the wall with his hand. It was no doubt a posada and some other traveller was trying for admittance. He heard again the sound of cautious knocking.

Next moment a broad band of light fell into the night through the opened door. Byrne stepped eagerly into it, whereupon the person outside leaped with a stifled cry away into the night. An exclamation of surprise was heard too, from within. Byrne, flinging himself against the half closed door, forced his way in against some considerable resistance.

A miserable candle, a mere rushlight, burned at the end of a long deal table. And in its light Byrne saw, staggering yet, the girl he had driven from the door. She had a short black skirt, an orange shawl, a dark complexion - and the escaped single hairs from the mass, sombre and thick like a forest and held up by a comb, made a black mist about her low forehead. A shrill lamentable howl of: "Misericordia!" came in two voices from the further end of the long room, where the fire-light of an open hearth played between heavy shadows. The girl recovering herself drew a hissing breath through her set teeth.

It is unnecessary to report the long process of questions and answers by which he soothed the fears of two old women who sat on each side of the fire, on which stood a large earthenware pot. Byrne thought at once of two witches watching the brewing of some deadly potion. But all the same, when one of them raising forward painfully her broken form lifted the cover of the pot, the escaping steam had an appetising smell. The other did not budge, but sat hunched up, her head trembling all the time.

They were horrible. There was something grotesque in their decrepitude. Their toothless mouths, their hooked noses, the meagreness of the active one, and the hanging yellow cheeks of the other (the still one, whose head trembled) would have been laughable if the sight of their dreadful physical degradation had not been appalling to one's eyes, had not gripped one's heart with poignant amazement at the unspeakable misery of age, at the awful persistency of life becoming at last an object of disgust and dread.

To get over it Byrne began to talk, saying that he was an Englishman, and that he was in search of a countryman who ought to have passed this way. Directly he had spoken the recollection of his parting with Tom came up in his mind with amazing vividness: the silent villagers, the angry gnome, the one-eyed wine-seller, Bernardino. Why! These two unspeakable frights must be that man's aunts - affiliated to the devil.

Whatever they had been once it was impossible to imagine what use such feeble creatures could be to the devil, now, in the world of the living. Which was Lucilla and which was Erminia? They were now things without a name. A moment of suspended animation followed Byrne's words. The sorceress with the spoon ceased stirring the mess in the iron pot, the very trembling of the other's head stopped for the space of breath. In this infinitesimal fraction of a second Byrne had the sense of being really on his quest, of having reached the turn of the path, almost within hail of Tom.

"They have seen him," he thought with conviction. Here was at last somebody who had seen him. He made sure they would deny all knowledge of the Ingles; but on the contrary they were eager to tell him that he had eaten and slept the night in the house. They both started talking together, describing his appearance and behaviour. An excitement quite fierce in its feebleness possessed them. The doubled-up sorceress flourished aloft her wooden spoon, the puffy monster got off her stool and screeched, stepping from one foot to the other, while the trembling of her head was accelerated to positive vibration. Byrne was quite disconcerted by their excited behaviour. . . Yes! The big, fierce Ingles went away in the morning, after eating a piece of bread and drinking some wine. And if the caballero wished to follow the same path nothing could be easier - in the morning.

"You will give me somebody to show me the way?" said Byrne.

"Si, senor. A proper youth. The man the caballero saw going out."

"But he was knocking at the door," protested Byrne. "He only bolted when he saw me. He was coming in."

"No! No!" the two horrid witches screamed out together. "Going out. Going out!"

After all it may have been true. The sound of knocking had been faint , elusive, reflected Byrne. Perhaps only the effect of his fancy. He asked -

"Who is that man?"

Joseph Conrad

"Her novio." They screamed pointing to the girl. "He is gone home to a village far away from here. But he will return in the morning. Her novio! And she is an orphan - the child of poor Christian people. She lives with us for the love of God, for the love of God."

The orphan crouching on the corner of the hearth had been looking at Byrne. He thought that she was more like a child of Satan kept there by these two weird harridans for the love of the Devil. Her eyes were a little oblique, her mouth rather thick, but admirably formed; her dark face had a wild beauty, voluptuous and untamed. As to the character of her steadfast gaze attached upon him with a sensuously savage attention, "to know what it was like," says Mr. Byrne, "you have only to observe a hungry cat watching a bird in a cage or a mouse inside a trap."

It was she who served him the food, of which he was glad; though with those big slanting black eyes examining him at close range, as if he had something curious written on his face, she gave him an uncomfortable sensation. But anything was better than being approached by these blear-eyed nightmarish witches. His apprehensions somehow had been soothed; perhaps by the sensation of warmth after severe exposure and the ease of resting after the exertion of fighting the gale inch by inch all the way. He had no doubt of Tom's safety. He was now sleeping in the mountain camp having been met by Gonzales' men.

Byrne rose, filled a tin goblet with wine out of a skin hanging on the wall, and sat down again. The witch with the mummy face began to talk to him, ramblingly of old times; she boasted of the inn's fame in those better days. Great people in their own coaches stopped there. An archbishop slept once in the casa, a long, long time ago.

The witch with the puffy face seemed to be listening from her stool, motionless, except for the trembling of her head. The girl (Byrne was certain she was a casual gipsy admitted there for some reason or other) sat on the hearth stone in the glow of the embers. She hummed a tune to herself, rattling a pair of castanets slightly now and then. At the mention of the archbishop she chuckled impiously and turned her head to look at Byrne, so that the red glow of the fire flashed in her black eyes and on her white teeth under the dark cowl of the enormous overmantel. And he smiled at her.

He rested now in the ease of security. His advent not having been expected there could be no plot against him in existence. Drowsiness stole upon his senses. He enjoyed it, but keeping a hold, so he thought at least, on his wits; but he must have been gone further than he thought because he was startled beyond measure by a fiendish uproar. He had never heard anything so pitilessly strident in his life. The witches had started a fierce quarrel about something or other. Whatever its origin they were now only abusing each other violently, without arguments; their senile screams expressed nothing but wicked anger and ferocious dismay. The gipsy girl's black eyes flew from one to the other. Never before had Byrne felt himself so removed from fellowship with human beings. Before he had really time to understand the subject of the quarrel, the girl jumped up rattling her castanets loudly. A silence fell. She came up to the table and bending over, her eyes in his -

"Senor," she said with decision, "You shall sleep in the archbishop's room."

Neither of the witches objected. The dried-up one bent double was propped on a stick. The puffy faced one had now a crutch.

Byrne got up, walked to the door, and turning the key in the enormous lock put it coolly in his pocket. This was clearly the only entrance, and he did not mean to be taken unawares by whatever danger there might have been lurking outside.

When he turned from the door he saw the two witches "affiliated to the Devil" and the Satanic girl looking at him in silence. He wondered if Tom Corbin took the same precaution last might. And thinking of him he had again that queer impression of his nearness. The world was perfectly dumb. And in this stillness he heard the blood beating in his ears with a confused rushing noise, in which there seemed to be a voice uttering the words: "Mr. Byrne, look out, sir." Tom's voice. He shuddered; for the delusions of the senses of hearing are the most vivid of all, and from their nature have a compelling character.

It seemed impossible that Tom should not be there. Again a slight chill as of stealthy draught penetrated through his very clothes and passed over all his body. He shook off the impression with an effort.

It was the girl who preceded him upstairs carrying an iron lamp from the naked flame of which ascended a thin thread of smoke. Her soiled white stockings were full of holes.

With the same quiet resolution with which he had locked the door below, Byrne threw open one after another the doors in the corridor. All the rooms were empty except for some nondescript lumber in one or two. And the girl seeing what he would be at stopped every time, raising the smoky light in each doorway patiently. Meantime she observed him with sustained attention. The last door of all she threw open herself.

"You sleep here, senor," she murmured in a voice light like a child's breath, offering him the lamp.

"Buenos noches, senorita," he said politely, taking it from her.

She didn't return the wish audibly, though her lips did move a little, while her gaze black like a starless night never for a moment wavered before him. He stepped in, and as he turned to close the door she was still there motionless and disturbing, with her voluptuous mouth and slanting eyes, with the expression of expectant sensual ferocity of a baffled cat. He hesitated for a moment, and in the dumb house he heard again the blood pulsating ponderously in his ears, while once more the illusion of Tom's voice speaking earnestly somewhere near by was specially terrifying, because this time he could not make out the words.

He slammed the door in the girl's face at last, leaving her in the dark; and he opened it again almost on the instant. Nobody. She had vanished without the slightest sound. He closed the door quickly and bolted it with two heavy bolts.

A profound mistrust possessed him suddenly. Why did the witches quarrel about letting him sleep here? And what meant that stare of the girl as if she wanted to impress his features for ever in her mind? His own nervousness alarmed him. He seemed to himself to be removed very far from mankind.

He examined his room. It was not very high, just high enough to take the bed which stood under an enormous baldaquin-like canopy from which fell heavy curtains at foot and head; a bed certainly worthy of an archbishop. There was a heavy table carved all round the edges, some arm-chairs of enormous weight like the spoils of a grandee's palace; a tall shallow wardrobe placed against the wall and with double doors. He tried them. Locked. A suspicion came into his mind, and he snatched the lamp to make a closer examination. No, it was not a disguised entrance. That heavy, tall piece of furniture stood clear of the wall by quite an inch. He glanced at the bolts of his room door. No! No one could get at him treacherously while he slept. But would he be able to sleep? he asked himself anxiously. If only he had Tom there - the trusty seaman who had fought at his right hand in a cutting out affair or two, and had always preached to him the necessity to take care of himself. "For it's no great trick," he used to say, "to get yourself killed in a hot fight. Any fool can do that. The proper pastime is to fight the Frenchies and then live to fight another day."

Byrne found it a hard matter not to fall into listening to the silence. Somehow he had the conviction that nothing would break it unless he heard again the haunting sound of Tom's voice. He had heard it twice before. Odd! And yet no wonder, he argued with himself reasonably, since he had been thinking of the man for over thirty hours continuously and, what's more, inconclusively. For his anxiety for Tom had never taken a definite shape. "Disappear," was the only word connected with the idea of Tom's danger. It was very vague and awful. "Disappear!" What did that mean?

Byrne shuddered, and then said to himself that he must be a little feverish. But Tom had not disappeared. Byrne had just heard of him. And again the young man felt the blood beating in his ears. He sat still expecting every moment to hear through the pulsating strokes the sound of Tom's voice. He waited straining his ears, but nothing came. Suddenly the thought occurred to him: "He has not disappeared, but he cannot make himself heard."

He jumped up from the arm-chair. How absurd! Laying his pistol and his hanger on the table he took off his boots and, feeling suddenly too tired to stand, flung himself on the bed which he found soft and comfortable beyond his hopes.

He had felt very wakeful, but he must have dozed off after all, because the next thing he knew he was sitting up in bed and trying to recollect what it was that Tom's voice had said. Oh! He remembered it now. It had said: "Mr. Byrne! Look out, sir!" A warning this. But against what?

He landed with one leap in the middle of the floor, gasped once, then looked all round the room. The window was shuttered and barred with an iron bar. Again he ran his eyes slowly all round the bare walls, and even looked up at the ceiling, which was rather high. Afterwards he went to the door to examine the fastenings. They consisted of two enormous iron bolts sliding into holes made in the wall; and as the corridor outside was too narrow to admit of any battering arrangement or even to permit an axe to be swung, nothing could burst the door open - unless gunpowder. But while he was still making sure that the lower bolt was pushed well home, he received the impression of somebody's presence in the room. It was so strong that he spun round quicker than lightning. There was no one. Who could there be? And yet . . .

It was then that he lost the decorum and restraint a man keeps up for his own sake. He got down on his hands and knees, with the lamp on the floor, to look under the bed, like a silly girl. He saw a lot of dust and nothing else. He got up, his cheeks burning, and walked about discontented with his own behaviour and unreasonably angry with Tom for not leaving him alone. The words: "Mr. Byrne! Look out, sir," kept on repeating themselves in his head in a tone of warning.

"Hadn't I better just throw myself on the bed and try to go to sleep," he asked himself. But his eyes fell on the tall wardrobe, and he went towards it feeling irritated with himself and yet unable to desist. How he could explain to-morrow the burglarious misdeed to the two odious witches he had no idea. Nevertheless he inserted the point of his hanger between the two halves of the door and tried to prize them open. They resisted. He swore, sticking now hotly to his purpose. His mutter: "I hope you will be satisfied, confound you," was addressed to the absent Tom. Just then the doors gave way and flew open.

He was there.

He - the trusty, sagacious, and courageous Tom was there, drawn up shadowy and stiff, in a prudent silence, which his wide-open eyes by their fixed gleam seemed to command Byrne to respect. But Byrne was too startled to make a sound. Amazed, he stepped back a little - and on the instant the seaman flung himself forward headlong as if to clasp his officer round the neck. Instinctively Byrne put out his faltering arms; he felt the horrible rigidity of the body and then the coldness of death as their heads knocked together and their faces came into contact. They reeled, Byrne hugging Tom close to his breast in order not to let him fall with a crash. He had just strength enough to lower the awful burden gently to the floor - then his head swam, his legs gave way, and he sank on his knees, leaning over the body with his hands resting on the breast of that man once full of generous life, and now as insensible as a stone.

"Dead! my poor Tom, dead," he repeated mentally. The light of the lamp standing near the edge of the table fell from above straight on the stony empty stare of these eyes which naturally had a mobile and merry expression.

Byrne turned his own away from them. Tom's black silk neckerchief was not knotted on his breast. It was gone. The murderers had also taken off his shoes and stockings. And noticing this spoliation, the exposed throat, the bare up-turned feet, Byrne felt his eyes run full of tears. In other respects the seaman was fully dressed; neither was his clothing disarranged as it must have been in a violent struggle. Only his checked shirt had been pulled a little out the waistband in one place, just enough to ascertain whether he had a money belt fastened round his body. Byrne began to sob into his handkerchief.

It was a nervous outburst which passed off quickly. Remaining on his knees he contemplated sadly the athletic body of as fine a seaman as ever had drawn a cutlass, laid a gun, or passed the weather earring in a gale, lying stiff and cold, his cheery, fearless spirit departed - perhaps turning to him, his boy chum, to his ship out there rolling on the grey seas off an iron-bound coast, at the very moment of its flight.

He perceived that the six brass buttons of Tom's jacket had been cut off. He shuddered at the notion of the two miserable and repulsive witches busying themselves ghoulishly about the defenceless body of his friend. Cut off. Perhaps with the same knife which . . . The head of one trembled; the other was bent double, and their eyes were red and bleared, their infamous claws unsteady. . . It must have been in this very room too, for Tom could not have been killed in the open and brought in here afterwards. Of that Byrne was certain. Yet those devilish crones could not have killed him themselves even by taking him unawares - and Tom would be always on his guard of course. Tom was a very wide awake wary man when engaged on any service. . . And in fact how did they murder him? Who did? In what way?

Byrne jumped up, snatched the lamp off the table, and stooped swiftly over the body. The light revealed on the clothing no stain, no trace, no spot of blood anywhere. Byrne's hands began to shake so that he had to set the lamp on the floor and turn away his head in order to recover from this agitation.

Then he began to explore that cold, still, and rigid body for a stab, a gunshot wound, for the trace of some killing blow. He felt all over the skull anxiously. It was whole. He slipped his hand under the neck. It was unbroken. With terrified eyes he peered close under the chin and saw no marks of strangulation on the throat.

There were no signs anywhere. He was just dead.

Impulsively Byrne got away from the body as if the mystery of an incomprehensible death had changed his pity into suspicion and dread. The lamp on the floor near the set, still face of the seaman showed it staring at the ceiling as if despairingly. In the circle of light Byrne saw by the undisturbed patches of thick dust on the floor that there had been no struggle in that room. "He has died outside," he thought. Yes, outside in that narrow corridor, where there was hardly room to turn, the mysterious death had come to his poor dear Tom. The impulse of snatching up his pistols and rushing out of the room abandoned Byrne suddenly. For Tom, too, had been armed - with just such powerless weapons as he himself possessed - pistols, a cutlass! And Tom had died a nameless death, by incomprehensible means.

A new thought came to Byrne. That stranger knocking at the door and fleeing so swiftly at his appearance had come there to remove the body. Aha! That was the guide the withered witch had promised would show the English officer the shortest way of rejoining his man. A promise, he saw it now, of dreadful import. He who had knocked would have two bodies to deal with. Man and officer would go forth from the house together. For Byrne was certain now that he would have to die before the morning - and in the same mysterious manner, leaving behind him an unmarked body.

The sight of a smashed head, of a throat cut, of a gaping gunshot wound, would have been an inexpressible relief. It would have soothed all his fears. His soul cried within him to that dead man whom he had never found wanting in danger. "Why don't you tell me what I am to look for, Tom? Why don't you?" But in rigid immobility, extended on his back, he seemed to preserve an austere silence, as if disdaining in the finality of his awful knowledge to hold converse with the living.

Suddenly Byrne flung himself on his knees by the side of the body, and dry-eyed, fierce, opened the shirt wide on the breast, as if to tear the secret forcibly from that cold heart which had been so loyal to him in life! Nothing! Nothing! He raised the lamp, and all the sign vouchsafed to him by that face which used to be so kindly in expression was a small bruise on the forehead - the least thing, a mere mark. The skin even was not broken. He stared at it a long time as if lost in a dreadful dream. Then he observed that Tom's hands were clenched as though he had fallen facing somebody in a fight with fists. His knuckles, on closer view, appeared somewhat abraded. Both hands.

The discovery of these slight signs was more appalling to Byrne than the absolute absence of every mark would have been. So Tom had died striking against something which could be hit, and yet could kill one without leaving a wound - by a breath.

Terror, hot terror, began to play about Byrne's heart like a tongue of flame that touches and withdraws before it turns a thing to ashes. He backed away from the body as far as he could, then came forward stealthily casting fearful glances to steal another look at the bruised forehead. There would perhaps be such a faint bruise on his own forehead - before the morning.

"I can't bear it," he whispered to himself. Tom was for him now an object of horror, a sight at once tempting and revolting to his fear. He couldn't bear to look at him.

At last, desperation getting the better of his increasing horror, he stepped forward from the wall against which he had been leaning, seized the corpse under the armpits, and began to lug it over to the bed. The bare heels of the seaman trailed on the floor noiselessly. He was heavy with the dead weight of inanimate objects. With a last effort Byrne landed him face downwards on the edge of the bed, rolled him over, snatched from under this stiff passive thing a sheet with which he covered it over. Then he spread the curtains at head and foot so that joining together as he shook their folds they hid the bed altogether from his sight.

He stumbled towards a chair, and fell on it. The perspiration poured from his face for a moment, and then his veins seemed to carry for a while a thin stream of half, frozen blood. Complete terror had possession of him now, a nameless terror which had turned his heart to ashes.

He sat upright in the straight-backed chair, the lamp burning at his feet, his pistols and his hanger at his left elbow on the end of the table, his eyes turning incessantly in their sockets round the walls, over the ceiling, over the floor, in the expectation of a mysterious and appalling vision. The thing which could deal death in a breath was outside that bolted door. But Byrne believed neither in walls nor bolts now. Unreasoning terror turning everything to account, his old time boyish admiration of the athletic Tom, the undaunted Tom (he had seemed to him invincible), helped to paralyse his faculties, added to his despair.

He was no longer Edgar Byrne. He was a tortured soul suffering more anguish than any sinner's body had ever suffered from rack or boot. The depth of his torment may be measured when I say that this young man, as brave at least as the average of his kind, contemplated seizing a pistol and firing into his own head. But a deadly, chilly, langour was spreading over his limbs. It was as if his flesh had been wet plaster stiffening slowly about his ribs. Presently, he thought, the two witches will be coming in, with crutch and stick - horrible, grotesque, monstrous - affiliated to the devil - to put a mark on his forehead, the tiny little bruise of death. And he wouldn't be able to do anything. Tom had struck out at something, but he was not like Tom. His limbs were dead already. He sat still, dying the death over and over again; and the only part of him which moved were his eyes, turning round and round in their sockets, running over the walls, the floor, the ceiling, again and again till suddenly they became motionless and stony-starting out of his head fixed in the direction of the bed.

He had seen the heavy curtains stir and shake as if the dead body they concealed had turned over and sat up. Byrne, who thought the world could hold no more terrors in store, felt his hair stir at the roots. He gripped the arms of the chair, his jaw fell, and the sweat broke out on his brow while his dry tongue clove suddenly to the roof of his mouth. Again the curtains stirred, but did not open. "Don't, Tom!" Byrne made effort to shout, but all he heard was a slight moan such as an uneasy sleeper may make. He felt that his brain was going, for, now, it seemed to him that the ceiling over the bed had moved, had slanted, and came level again -

and once more the closed curtains swayed gently as if about to part.

Byrne closed his eyes not to see the awful apparition of the seaman's corpse coming out animated by an evil spirit. In the profound silence of the room he endured a moment of frightful agony, then opened his eyes again. And he saw at once that the curtains remained closed still, but that the ceiling over the bed had risen quite a foot. With the last gleam of reason left to him he understood that it was the enormous baldaquin over the bed which was coming down, while the curtains attached to it swayed softly, sinking gradually to the floor. His drooping jaw snapped to - and half rising in his chair he watched mutely the noiseless descent of the monstrous canopy. It came down in short smooth rushes till lowered half way or more, when it took a run and settled swiftly its turtle-back shape with the deep border piece fitting exactly the edge of the bedstead. A slight crack or two of wood were heard, and the overpowering stillness of the room resumed its sway.

Byrne stood up, gasped for breath, and let out a cry of rage and dismay, the first sound which he is perfectly certain did make its way past his lips on this night of terrors. This then was the death he had escaped! This was the devilish artifice of murder poor Tom's soul had perhaps tried from beyond the border to warn him of. For this was how he had died. Byrne was certain he had heard the voice of the seaman, faintly distinct in his familiar phrase, "Mr. Byrne! Look out, sir!" and again uttering words he could not make out. But then the distance separating the living from the dead is so great! Poor Tom had tried. Byrne ran to the bed and attempted to lift up, to push off the horrible lid smothering the body. It resisted his efforts, heavy as lead, immovable like a tombstone. The rage of vengeance made him desist; his head buzzed with chaotic thoughts of extermination, he turned round the room as if he could find neither his weapons nor the way out; and all the time he stammered awful menaces. . .

A violent battering at the door of the inn recalled him to his soberer senses. He flew to the window pulled the shutters open, and looked out. In the faint dawn he saw below him a mob of men. Ha! He would go and face at once this murderous lot collected no doubt for his undoing. After his struggle with nameless terrors he yearned for an open fray with armed enemies. But he must have remained yet bereft of his reason, because forgetting his weapons he rushed downstairs with a wild cry, unbarred the door while blows were raining on it outside, and flinging it open flew with his bare hands at the throat of the first man he saw before him. They rolled over together. Byrne's hazy intention was to break through, to fly up the mountain path, and come back presently with Gonzales' men to exact an exemplary vengeance. He fought furiously till a tree, a house, a mountain, seemed to crash down upon his head - and he knew no more.

* * * * *

Here Mr. Byrne describes in detail the skilful manner in which he found his broken head bandaged, informs us that he had lost a great deal of blood, and ascribes the preservation of his sanity to that circumstance. He sets down Gonzales' profuse apologies in full too. For it was Gonzales who, tired of waiting for news from the English, had come down to the inn with half his band, on his way to the sea. "His excellency," he explained, "rushed out with fierce impetuosity, and, moreover, was not known to us for a friend, and so we etc., etc. When asked what had become of the witches, he only pointed his finger silently to the ground, then voiced calmly a moral reflection: "The passion for gold is pitiless in the very old, senor," he said. "No doubt in former days they have put many a solitary traveller to sleep in the archbishop's bed."

"There was also a gipsy girl there," said Byrne feebly from the improvised litter on which he was being carried to the coast by a squad of guerilleros.

"It was she who winched up that infernal machine, and it was she too who lowered it that night," was the answer.

"But why? Why?" exclaimed Byrne. "Why should she wish for my death?"

"No doubt for the sake of your excellency's coat buttons," said politely the saturnine Gonzales. "We found those of the dead mariner concealed on her person. But your excellency may rest assured that everything that is fitting has been done on this occasion."

Byrne asked no more questions. There was still another death which was considered by Gonzales as "fitting to the occasion." The one-eyed Bernardino stuck against the wall of his wine-shop received the charge of six escopettas into his breast. As the shots rang out the rough bier with Tom's body on it went past carried by a bandit-like gang of Spanish patriots down the ravine to the shore, where two boats from the ship were waiting for what was left on earth of her best seaman.

Mr. Byrne, very pale and weak, stepped into the boat which carried the body of his humble friend. For it was decided that Tom Corbin should rest far out in the bay of Biscay. The officer took the tiller and, turning his head for the last look at the shore, saw on the grey hillside something moving, which he made out to be a little man in a yellow hat mounted on a mule - that mule without which the fate of Tom Corbin would have remained mysterious for ever.

June, 1913.

BECAUSE OF THE DOLLARS

CHAPTER I

While we were hanging about near the water's edge, as sailors idling ashore will do (it was in the open space before the Harbour Office of a great Eastern port), a man came towards us from the "front" of business houses, aiming obliquely at the landing steps. He attracted my attention because in the movement of figures in white drill suits on the pavement from which he stepped, his costume, the usual tunic and trousers, being made of light grey flannel, made him noticeable.

I had time to observe him. He was stout, but he was not grotesque. His face was round and smooth, his complexion very fair. On his nearer approach I saw a little moustache made all the fairer by a good many white hairs. And he had, for a stout man, quite a good chin. In passing us he exchanged nods with the friend I was with and smiled.

My friend was Hollis, the fellow who had so many adventures and had known so many queer people in that part of the (more or less) gorgeous East in the days of his youth. He said: "That's a good man. I don't mean good in the sense of smart or skilful in his trade. I mean a really GOOD man."

Joseph Conrad

I turned round at once to look at the phenomenon. The "really GOOD man" had a very broad back. I saw him signal a sampan to come alongside, get into it, and go off in the direction of a cluster of local steamers anchored close inshore.

I said: "He's a seaman, isn't he?"

"Yes. Commands that biggish dark-green steamer: 'Sissie - Glasgow.' He has never commanded anything else but the 'Sissie - Glasgow,' only it wasn't always the same Sissie. The first he had was about half the length of this one, and we used to tell poor Davidson that she was a size too small for him. Even at that time Davidson had bulk. We warned him he would get callosities on his shoulders and elbows because of the tight fit of his command. And Davidson could well afford the smiles he gave us for our chaff. He made lots of money in her. She belonged to a portly Chinaman resembling a mandarin in a picture-book, with goggles and thin drooping moustaches, and as dignified as only a Celestial knows how to be.

"The best of Chinamen as employers is that they have such gentlemanly instincts. Once they become convinced that you are a straight man, they give you their unbounded confidence. You simply can't do wrong, then. And they are pretty quick judges of character, too. Davidson's Chinaman was the first to find out his worth, on some theoretical principle. One day in his counting-house, before several white men he was heard to declare: 'Captain Davidson is a good man.' And that settled it. After that you couldn't tell if it was Davidson who belonged to the Chinaman or the Chinaman who belonged to Davidson. It was he who, shortly before he died, ordered in Glasgow the new

Sissie for Davidson to command."

We walked into the shade of the Harbour Office and leaned our elbows on the parapet of the quay.

"She was really meant to comfort poor Davidson," continued Hollis. "Can you fancy anything more naively touching than this old mandarin spending several thousand pounds to console his white man? Well, there she is. The old mandarin's sons have inherited her, and Davidson with her; and he commands her; and what with his salary and trading privileges he makes a lot of money; and everything is as before; and Davidson even smiles - you have seen it? Well, the smile's the only thing which isn't as before."

"Tell me, Hollis," I asked, "what do you mean by good in this connection?"

"Well, there are men who are born good just as others are born witty. What I mean is his nature. No simpler, more scrupulously delicate soul had ever lived in such a - a - comfortable envelope. How we used to laugh at Davidson's fine scruples! In short, he's thoroughly humane, and I don't imagine there can be much of any other sort of goodness that counts on this earth. And as he's that with a shade of particular refinement, I may well call him a 'REALLY good man.'"

I knew from old that Hollis was a firm believer in the final value of shades. And I said: "I see" - because I really did see Hollis's Davidson in the sympathetic stout man who had passed us a little while before. But I remembered that at the very moment he smiled his placid face appeared veiled in melancholy - a sort of spiritual shadow. I went on.

"Who on earth has paid him off for being so fine by spoiling his smile?"

"That's quite a story, and I will tell it to you if you like. Confound it! It's quite a surprising one, too. Surprising in every way, but mostly in the way it knocked over poor Davidson - and apparently only because he is such a good sort. He was telling me all about it only a few days ago. He said that when he saw these four fellows with their heads in a bunch over the table, he at once didn't like it. He didn't like it at all. You mustn't suppose that Davidson is a soft fool. These men -

"But I had better begin at the beginning. We must go back to the first time the old dollars had been called in by our Government in exchange for a new issue. Just about the time when I left these parts to go home for a long stay. Every trader in the islands was thinking of getting his old dollars sent up here in time, and the demand for empty French wine cases - you know the dozen of vermouth or claret size - was something unprecedented. The custom was to pack the dollars in little bags of a hundred each. I don't know how many bags each case would hold. A good lot. Pretty tidy sums must have been moving afloat just then. But let us get away from here. Won't do to stay in the sun. Where could we - ? I know! Let us go to those tiffin-rooms over there."

We moved over accordingly. Our appearance in the long empty room at that early hour caused visible consternation amongst the China boys. But Hollis led the way to one of the tables between the windows screened by rattan blinds. A brilliant half-light trembled on the ceiling, on the whitewashed walls, bathed the multitude of vacant chairs and tables in a peculiar, stealthy glow.

"All right. We will get something to eat when it's ready," he said, waving the anxious Chinaman waiter aside. He took his temples touched with grey between his hands, leaning over the table to bring his face, his dark, keen eyes, closer to mine.

"Davidson then was commanding the steamer Sissie - the little one which we used to chaff him about. He ran her alone, with only the Malay serang for a deck officer. The nearest approach to another white man on board of her was the engineer, a Portuguese half-caste, as thin as a lath and quite a youngster at that. For all practical purposes Davidson was managing that command of his single-handed; and of course this was known in the port. I am telling you of it because the fact had its influence on the developments you shall hear of presently.

"His steamer, being so small, could go up tiny creeks and into shallow bays and through reefs and over sand-banks, collecting produce, where no other vessel but a native craft would think of venturing. It is a paying game, often. Davidson was known to visit in her places that no one else could find and that hardly anybody had ever heard of.

"The old dollars being called in, Davidson's Chinaman thought that the Sissie would be just the thing to collect them from small traders in the less frequented parts of the Archipelago. It's a good business. Such cases of dollars are dumped aft in the ship's lazarette, and you get good freight for very little trouble and space.

"Davidson, too, thought it was a good idea; and together they made up a list of his calls on his next trip. Then Davidson (he had naturally the chart of his voyages in his head) remarked that on his way back he might look in at a certain settlement up a mere creek, where a poor sort of white man lived in a native village. Davidson pointed out to his Chinaman that the fellow was certain to have some rattans to ship.

"'Probably enough to fill her forward,' said Davidson. 'And that'll be better than bringing her back with empty holds. A day more or less doesn't matter.'

"This was sound talk, and the Chinaman owner could not but agree. But if it hadn't been sound it would have been just the same. Davidson did what he liked. He was a man that could do no wrong. However, this suggestion of his was not merely a business matter. There was in it a touch of Davidsonian kindness. For you must know that the man could not have continued to live quietly up that creek if it had not been for Davidson's willingness to call there from time to time. And Davidson's Chinaman knew this perfectly well, too. So he only smiled his dignified, bland smile, and said: 'All right, Captain. You do what you like.'

"I will explain presently how this connection between Davidson and that fellow came about. Now I want to tell you about the part of this affair which happened here - the preliminaries of it.

"You know as well as I do that these tiffin-rooms where we are sitting now have been in existence for many years. Well, next day about twelve o'clock, Davidson dropped in here to get something to eat.

"And here comes the only moment in this story where accident - mere accident - plays a part. If Davidson had gone home that day for tiffin, there would be now, after twelve years or more, nothing changed in his kindly, placid smile.

"But he came in here; and perhaps it was sitting at this very table that he remarked to a friend of mine that his next trip was to be a dollar-collecting trip. He added, laughing, that his wife was making rather a fuss about it. She had begged him to stay ashore and get somebody else to take his place for a voyage. She thought there was some danger on account of the dollars. He told her, he said, that there were no Java-sea pirates nowadays except in boys' books. He had laughed at her fears, but he was very sorry, too; for when she took any notion in her head it was impossible to argue her out of it. She would be worrying herself all the time he was away. Well, he couldn't help it. There was no one ashore fit to take his place for the trip.

"This friend of mine and I went home together in the same mail-boat, and he mentioned that conversation one evening in the Red Sea while we were talking over the things and people we had just left, with more or less regret.

"I can't say that Davidson occupied a very prominent place. Moral excellence seldom does. He was quietly appreciated by those who knew him well; but his more obvious distinction consisted in this, that he was married. Ours, as you remember, was a bachelor crowd; in spirit anyhow, if not absolutely in fact. There might have been a few wives in existence, but if so they were invisible, distant, never alluded to. For what would have been the good? Davidson alone was visibly married.

"Being married suited him exactly. It fitted him so well that the wildest of us did not resent the fact when it was disclosed. Directly he had felt his feet out here, Davidson sent for his wife. She came out (from West Australia) in the Somerset, under the care of Captain Ritchie - you know, Monkey-face Ritchie - who couldn't praise enough her sweetness, her gentleness, and her charm. She seemed to be the heaven-born mate for Davidson. She found on arrival a very pretty bungalow on the hill, ready for her and the little girl they had. Very soon he got for her a two-wheeled trap and a Burmah pony, and she used to drive down of an evening to pick up Davidson, on the quay. When Davidson, beaming, got into the trap, it would become very full all at once.

"We used to admire Mrs. Davidson from a distance. It was a girlish head out of a keepsake. From a distance. We had not many opportunities for a closer view, because she did not care to give them to us. We would have been glad to drop in at the Davidson bungalow, but we were made to feel somehow that we were not very welcome there. Not that she ever said anything ungracious. She never had much to say for herself. I was perhaps the one who saw most of the Davidsons at home. What I noticed under the superficial aspect of vapid sweetness was her convex, obstinate forehead, and her small, red, pretty, ungenerous mouth. But then I am an observer with strong prejudices. Most of us were fetched by her white, swan-like neck, by that drooping, innocent profile. There was a lot of latent devotion to Davidson's wife hereabouts, at that time, I can tell you. But my idea was that she repaid it by a profound suspicion of the sort of men we were; a mistrust which extended - I fancied - to her very husband at times. And I thought then she was jealous of him in a way; though there were no women that she could be jealous about. She had no women's society. It's difficult for a shipmaster's wife unless there are other shipmasters' wives about, and there were none here then. I know that the dock manager's wife called on her; but that was all. The fellows here formed the opinion that Mrs. Davidson was a meek, shy little thing. She looked it, I must say. And this opinion was so universal that the friend I have been telling you of remembered his conversation with Davidson simply because of the statement about Davidson's wife. He even wondered to me: 'Fancy Mrs. Davidson making a fuss to that extent. She didn't seem to me the sort of woman that would know how to make a fuss about anything.'

"I wondered, too - but not so much. That bumpy forehead - eh? I had always suspected her of being silly. And I observed that Davidson must have been vexed by this display of wifely anxiety.

"My friend said: 'No. He seemed rather touched and distressed. There really was no one he could ask to relieve him; mainly because he intended to make a call in some God-forsaken creek, to look up a fellow of the name of Bamtz who apparently had settled there.'

"And again my friend wondered. 'Tell me,' he cried, 'what connection can there be between Davidson and such a creature as Bamtz?'

"I don't remember now what answer I made. A sufficient one could have been given in two words: 'Davidson's goodness.' THAT never boggled at unworthiness if there was the slightest reason for compassion. I don't want you to think that Davidson had no discrimination at all. Bamtz could not have imposed on him. Moreover, everybody knew what Bamtz was. He was a loafer with a beard. When I think of Bamtz, the first thing I see is that long black beard and a lot of propitiatory wrinkles at the corners of two little eyes. There was no such beard from here to Polynesia, where a beard is a valuable property in itself. Bamtz's beard was valuable to him in another way. You know how impressed Orientals are by a fine beard. Years and years ago, I remember, the grave Abdullah, the great trader of Sambir, unable to repress signs of astonishment and admiration at the first sight of that imposing beard. And it's very well known that Bamtz lived on Abdullah off and on for several years. It was a unique beard, and so was the bearer of the same. A unique loafer. He made a fine art of it, or rather a sort of craft and mystery. One can understand a fellow living by cadging and small swindles in towns, in large communities of people; but Bamtz managed to do that trick in the wilderness, to loaf on the outskirts of the virgin forest.

"He understood how to ingratiate himself with the natives. He would arrive in some settlement up a river, make a present of a cheap carbine or a pair of shoddy binoculars, or something of that sort, to the Rajah, or the head-man, or the principal trader; and on the strength of that gift, ask for a house, posing mysteriously as a very special trader. He would spin them no end of yarns, live on the fat of the land, for a while, and then do some mean swindle or other - or else they would get tired of him and ask him to quit. And he would go off meekly with an air of injured innocence. Funny life. Yet, he never got hurt somehow. I've heard of the Rajah of Dongala giving him fifty dollars' worth of trade goods and paying his passage in a prau only to get rid of him. Fact. And observe that nothing prevented the old fellow having Bamtz's throat cut and the carcase thrown into deep water outside the reefs; for who on earth would have inquired after Bamtz?

"He had been known to loaf up and down the wilderness as far north as the Gulf of Tonkin. Neither did he disdain a spell of civilisation from time to time. And it was while loafing and cadging in Saigon, bearded and dignified (he gave himself out there as a bookkeeper), that he came across Laughing Anne.

"The less said of her early history the better, but something must be said. We may safely suppose there was very little heart left in her famous laugh when Bamtz spoke first to her in some low cafe. She was stranded in Saigon with precious little money and in great trouble about a kid she had, a boy of five or six.

"A fellow I just remember, whom they called Pearler Harry, brought her out first into these parts - from Australia, I believe. He brought her out and then dropped her, and she remained knocking about here and there, known to most of us by sight, at any rate. Everybody in the Archipelago had heard of Laughing Anne. She had really a pleasant silvery laugh always at her disposal, so to speak, but it wasn't enough apparently to make her fortune. The poor creature was ready to stick to any half-decent man if he would only let her, but she always got dropped, as it might have been expected.

"She had been left in Saigon by the skipper of a German ship with whom she had been going up and down the China coast as far as Vladivostok for near upon two years. The German said to her: 'This is all over, mein Taubchen. I am going home now to get married to the girl I got engaged to before coming out here.' And Anne said: 'All right, I'm ready to go. We part friends, don't we?'

"She was always anxious to part friends. The German told her that of course they were parting friends. He looked rather glum at the moment of parting. She laughed and went ashore.

"But it was no laughing matter for her. She had some notion that this would be her last chance. What frightened her most was the future of her child. She had left her boy in Saigon before going off with the German, in the care of an elderly French couple. The husband was a doorkeeper in some Government office, but his time was up, and they were returning to France. She had to take the boy back from them; and after she had got him back, she did not like to part with him any more.

"That was the situation when she and Bamtz got acquainted casually. She could not have had any illusions about that fellow. To pick up with Bamtz was coming down pretty low in the world, even from a material point of view. She had always been decent, in her way; whereas Bamtz was, not to mince words, an abject sort of creature. On the other hand, that bearded loafer, who looked much more like a pirate than a bookkeeper, was not a brute. He was gentle - rather -

even in his cups. And then, despair, like misfortune, makes us acquainted with strange bed-fellows. For she may well have despaired. She was no longer young - you know.

"On the man's side this conjunction is more difficult to explain, perhaps. One thing, however, must be said of Bamtz; he had always kept clear of native women. As one can't suspect him of moral delicacy, I surmise that it must have been from prudence. And he, too, was no longer young. There were many white hairs in his valuable black beard by then. He may have simply longed for some kind of companionship in his queer, degraded existence. Whatever their motives, they vanished from Saigon together. And of course nobody cared what had become of them.

"Six months later Davidson came into the Mirrah Settlement. It was the very first time he had been up that creek, where no European vessel had ever been seen before. A Javanese passenger he had on board offered him fifty dollars to call in there - it must have been some very particular business - and Davidson consented to try. Fifty dollars, he told me, were neither here nor there; but he was curious to see the place, and the little Sissie could go anywhere where there was water enough to float a soup-plate.

"Davidson landed his Javanese plutocrat, and, as he had to wait a couple of hours for the tide, he went ashore himself to stretch his legs.

"It was a small settlement. Some sixty houses, most of them built on piles over the river, the rest scattered in the long grass; the usual pathway at the back; the forest hemming in the clearing and smothering what there might have been of air into a dead, hot stagnation.

"All the population was on the river-bank staring silently, as Malays will do, at the Sissie anchored in the stream. She was almost as wonderful to them as an angel's visit. Many of the old people had only heard vaguely of fire-ships, and not many of the younger generation had seen one. On the back path Davidson strolled in perfect solitude. But he became aware of a bad smell and concluded he would go no farther.

"While he stood wiping his forehead, he heard from somewhere the exclamation: 'My God! It's Davy!'

"Davidson's lower jaw, as he expressed it, came unhooked at the crying of this excited voice. Davy was the name used by the associates of his young days; he hadn't heard it for many years. He stared about with his mouth open and saw a white woman issue from the long grass in which a small hut stood buried nearly up to the roof.

"Try to imagine the shock: in that wild place that you couldn't find on a map, and more squalid than the most poverty-stricken Malay settlement had a right to be, this European woman coming swishing out of the long grass in a fanciful tea-gown thing, dingy pink satin, with a long train and frayed lace trimmings; her eyes like black coals in a pasty-white face. Davidson thought that he was asleep, that he was delirious. From the offensive village mudhole (it was what Davidson had sniffed just before) a couple of filthy buffaloes uprose with loud snorts and lumbered off crashing through the bushes, panic-struck by this apparition.

"The woman came forward, her arms extended, and

laid her hands on Davidson's shoulders, exclaiming: 'Why! You have hardly changed at all. The same good Davy.' And she laughed a little wildly.

"This sound was to Davidson like a galvanic shock to a corpse. He started in every muscle. 'Laughing Anne,' he said in an awe-struck voice.

"'All that's left of her, Davy. All that's left of her.'

"Davidson looked up at the sky; but there was to be seen no balloon from which she could have fallen on that spot. When he brought his distracted gaze down, it rested on a child holding on with a brown little paw to the pink satin gown. He had run out of the grass after her. Had Davidson seen a real hobgoblin his eyes could not have bulged more than at this small boy in a dirty white blouse and ragged knickers. He had a round head of tight chestnut curls, very sunburnt legs, a freckled face, and merry eyes. Admonished by his mother to greet the gentleman, he finished off Davidson by addressing him in French.

"'Bonjour.'

"Davidson, overcome, looked up at the woman in silence. She sent the child back to the hut, and when he had disappeared in the grass, she turned to Davidson, tried to speak, but after getting out the words, 'That's my Tony,' burst into a long fit of crying. She had to lean on Davidson's shoulder. He, distressed in the goodness of his heart, stood rooted to the spot where she had come upon him.

"What a meeting - eh? Bamtz had sent her out to see what white man it was who had landed. And she had recognised him from that time when Davidson, who had been pearling himself in his youth, had been associating with Harry the Pearler and others, the quietest of a rather rowdy set.

"Before Davidson retraced his steps to go on board the steamer, he had heard much of Laughing Anne's story, and had even had an interview, on the path, with Bamtz himself. She ran back to the hut to fetch him, and he came out lounging, with his hands in his pockets, with the detached, casual manner under which he concealed his propensity to cringe. Ya-a-as-as. He thought he would settle here permanently - with her. This with a nod at Laughing Anne, who stood by, a haggard, tragically anxious figure, her black hair hanging over her shoulders.

"'No more paint and dyes for me, Davy,' she struck in, 'if only you will do what he wants you to do. You know that I was always ready to stand by my men - if they had only let me.'

"Davidson had no doubt of her earnestness. It was of Bamtz's good faith that he was not at all sure. Bamtz wanted Davidson to promise to call at Mirrah more or less regularly. He thought he saw an opening to do business with rattans there, if only he could depend on some craft to bring out trading goods and take away his produce.

"'I have a few dollars to make a start on. The people are all right.'

"He had come there, where he was not known, in a native prau, and had managed, with his sedate manner and the exactly right kind of yarn he knew how to tell to the natives, to ingratiate himself with the chief man.

"'The Orang Kaya has given me that empty house there to live in as long as I will stay,' added Bamtz.

"'Do it, Davy,' cried the woman suddenly. 'Think of that poor kid.'

"'Seen him? 'Cute little customer,' said the reformed loafer in such a tone of interest as to surprise Davidson into a kindly glance.

"'I certainly can do it,' he declared. He thought of at first making some stipulation as to Bamtz behaving decently to the woman, but his exaggerated delicacy and also the conviction that such a fellow's promises were worth nothing restrained him. Anne went a little distance down the path with him talking anxiously.

"'It's for the kid. How could I have kept him with me if I had to knock about in towns? Here he will never know that his mother was a painted woman. And this Bamtz likes him. He's real fond of him. I suppose I ought to thank God for that.'

"Davidson shuddered at any human creature being brought so low as to have to thank God for the favours or affection of a Bamtz.

"'And do you think that you can make out to live here?' he asked gently.

"'Can't I? You know I have always stuck to men through thick and thin till they had enough of me. And now look at me! But inside I am as I always was. I have acted on the square to them all one after another.

Only they do get tired somehow. Oh, Davy! Harry ought not to have cast me off. It was he that led me astray.'

"Davidson mentioned to her that Harry the Pearler had been dead now for some years. Perhaps she had heard?

"She made a sign that she had heard; and walked by the side of Davidson in silence nearly to the bank. Then she told him that her meeting with him had brought back the old times to her mind. She had not cried for years. She was not a crying woman either. It was hearing herself called Laughing Anne that had started her sobbing like a fool. Harry was the only man she had loved. The others -

"She shrugged her shoulders. But she prided herself on her loyalty to the successive partners of her dismal adventures. She had never played any tricks in her life. She was a pal worth having. But men did get tired. They did not understand women. She supposed it had to be.

"Davidson was attempting a veiled warning as to Bamtz, but she interrupted him. She knew what men were. She knew what this man was like. But he had taken wonderfully to the kid. And Davidson desisted willingly, saying to himself that surely poor Laughing Anne could have no illusions by this time. She wrung his hand hard at parting.

"'It's for the kid, Davy - it's for the kid. Isn't he a bright little chap?'

CHAPTER II

"All this happened about two years before the day when Davidson, sitting in this very room, talked to my friend. You will see presently how this room can get full. Every seat'll be occupied, and as you notice, the tables are set close, so that the backs of the chairs are almost touching. There is also a good deal of noisy talk here about one o'clock.

"I don't suppose Davidson was talking very loudly; but very likely he had to raise his voice across the table to my friend. And here accident, mere accident, put in its work by providing a pair of fine ears close behind Davidson's chair. It was ten to one against, the owner of the same having enough change in his pockets to get his tiffin here. But he had. Most likely had rooked somebody of a few dollars at cards overnight. He was a bright creature of the name of Fector, a spare, short, jumpy fellow with a red face and muddy eyes. He described himself as a journalist as certain kind of women give themselves out as actresses in the dock of a police-court.

"He used to introduce himself to strangers as a man with a mission to track out abuses and fight them whenever found. He would also hint that he was a martyr. And it's a fact that he had been kicked, horsewhipped, imprisoned, and hounded with ignominy out of pretty well every place between Ceylon and Shanghai, for a professional blackmailer.

"I suppose, in that trade, you've got to have active wits and sharp ears. It's not likely that he overheard every word Davidson said about his dollar collecting trip, but he heard enough to set his wits at work.

"He let Davidson go out, and then hastened away down to the native slums to a sort of lodging-house kept in partnership by the usual sort of Portuguese and a very disreputable Chinaman. Macao Hotel, it was called, but it was mostly a gambling den that one used to warn fellows against. Perhaps you remember?

"There, the evening before, Fector had met a precious couple, a partnership even more queer than the Portuguese and the Chinaman. One of the two was Niclaus - you know. Why! the fellow with a Tartar moustache and a yellow complexion, like a Mongolian, only that his eyes were set straight and his face was not so flat. One couldn't tell what breed he was. A nondescript beggar. From a certain angle you would think a very bilious white man. And I daresay he was. He owned a Malay prau and called himself The Nakhoda, as one would say: The Captain. Aha! Now you remember. He couldn't, apparently, speak any other European language than English, but he flew the Dutch flag on his prau.

"The other was the Frenchman without hands. Yes. The very same we used to know in '79 in Sydney, keeping a little tobacco shop at the lower end of George Street. You remember the huge carcase hunched up behind the counter, the big white face and the long black hair brushed back off a high forehead like a bard's. He was always trying to roll cigarettes on his knee with his stumps, telling endless yarns of Polynesia and whining and cursing in turn about 'mon malheur.' His hands had been blown away by a dynamite cartridge while fishing in some lagoon. This accident, I believe, had made him more wicked than before, which is saying a good deal.

"He was always talking about 'resuming his activities' some day, whatever they were, if he could only get an intelligent companion. It was evident that the little shop was no field for his activities, and the sickly woman with her face tied up, who used to look in sometimes through the back door, was no companion for him.

"And, true enough, he vanished from Sydney before long, after some trouble with the Excise fellows about his stock. Goods stolen out of a warehouse or something similar. He left the woman behind, but he must have secured some sort of companion - he could not have shifted for himself; but whom he went away with, and where, and what other companions he might have picked up afterwards, it is impossible to make the remotest guess about.

"Why exactly he came this way I can't tell. Towards the end of my time here we began to hear talk of a maimed Frenchman who had been seen here and there. But no one knew then that he had foregathered with Niclaus and lived in his prau. I daresay he put Niclaus up to a thing or two. Anyhow, it was a partnership. Niclaus was somewhat afraid of the Frenchman on account of his tempers, which were awful. He looked then like a devil; but a man without hands, unable to load or handle a weapon, can at best go for one only with his teeth. From that danger Niclaus felt certain he could always defend himself.

"The couple were alone together loafing in the common-room of that infamous hotel when Fector turned up. After some beating about the bush, for he was doubtful how far he could trust these two, he repeated what he had overheard in the tiffin-rooms.

"His tale did not have much success till he came to mention the creek and Bamtz's name. Niclaus, sailing about like a native in a prau, was, in his own words, 'familiar with the locality.' The huge Frenchman, walking up and down the room with his stumps in the pockets of his jacket, stopped short in surprise. 'Comment? Bamtz! Bamtz!'

"He had run across him several times in his life. He exclaimed: 'Bamtz! Mais je ne connais que ca!' And he applied such a contemptuously indecent epithet to Bamtz that when, later, he alluded to him as 'une chiffe' (a mere rag) it sounded quite complimentary. 'We can do with him what we like,' he asserted confidently. 'Oh, yes. Certainly we must hasten to pay a visit to that - ' (another awful descriptive epithet quite unfit for repetition). 'Devil take me if we don't pull off a coup that will set us all up for a long time.'

"He saw all that lot of dollars melted into bars and disposed of somewhere on the China coast. Of the escape after the coup he never doubted. There was Niclaus's prau to manage that in.

"In his enthusiasm he pulled his stumps out of his pockets and waved them about. Then, catching sight of them, as it were, he held them in front of his eyes, cursing and blaspheming and bewailing his misfortune and his helplessness, till Niclaus quieted him down.

"But it was his mind that planned out the affair and it was his spirit which carried the other two on. Neither of them was of the bold buccaneer type; and Fector, especially, had never in his adventurous life used other weapons than slander and lies.

"That very evening they departed on a visit to Bamtz in Niclaus's prau, which had been lying, emptied of her cargo of cocoanuts, for a day or two under the canal bridge. They must have crossed the bows of the anchored Sissie, and no doubt looked at her with interest as the scene of their future exploit, the great haul, le grand coup!

"Davidson's wife, to his great surprise, sulked with him for several days before he left. I don't know whether it occurred to him that, for all her angelic profile, she was a very stupidly obstinate girl. She didn't like the tropics. He had brought her out there, where she had no friends, and now, she said, he was becoming inconsiderate. She had a presentiment of some misfortune, and notwithstanding Davidson's pain-staking explanations, she could not see why her presentiments were to be disregarded. On the very last evening before Davidson went away she asked him in a suspicious manner:

"'Why is it that you are so anxious to go this time?'

"'I am not anxious,' protested the good Davidson. 'I simply can't help myself. There's no one else to go in my place.'

"'Oh! There's no one,' she said, turning away slowly.

"She was so distant with him that evening that Davidson from a sense of delicacy made up his mind to say good-bye to her at once and go and sleep on board. He felt very miserable and, strangely enough, more on his own account than on account of his wife. She seemed to him much more offended than grieved.

"Three weeks later, having collected a good many cases of old dollars (they were stowed aft in the lazarette with an iron bar and a padlock securing the hatch under his cabin-table), yes, with a bigger lot than he had expected to collect, he found himself homeward bound and off the entrance of the creek where Bamtz lived and even, in a sense, flourished.

"It was so late in the day that Davidson actually hesitated whether he should not pass by this time. He had no regard for Bamtz, who was a degraded but not a really unhappy man. His pity for Laughing Anne was no more than her case deserved. But his goodness was of a particularly delicate sort. He realised how these people were dependent on him, and how they would feel their dependence (if he failed to turn up) through a long month of anxious waiting. Prompted by his sensitive humanity, Davidson, in the gathering dusk, turned the Sissie's head towards the hardly discernible coast, and navigated her safety through a maze of shallow patches. But by the time he got to the mouth of the creek the night had come.

"The narrow waterway lay like a black cutting through the forest. And as there were always grounded snaggs in the channel which it would be impossible to make out, Davidson very prudently turned the Sissie round, and with only enough steam on the boilers to give her a touch ahead if necessary, let her drift up stern first with the tide, silent and invisible in the impenetrable darkness and in the dumb stillness.

"It was a long job, and when at the end of two hours Davidson thought he must be up to the clearing, the settlement slept already, the whole land of forests and rivers was asleep.

"Davidson, seeing a solitary light in the massed darkness of the shore, knew that it was burning in Bamtz's house. This was unexpected at this time of the night, but convenient as a guide. By a turn of the screw and a touch of the helm he sheered the Sissie alongside Bamtz's wharf - a miserable structure of a dozen piles and a few planks, of which the ex-vagabond was very proud. A couple of Kalashes jumped down on it, took a turn with the ropes thrown to them round the posts, and the Sissie came to rest without a single loud word or the slightest noise. And just in time too, for the tide turned even before she was properly moored.

"Davidson had something to eat, and then, coming on deck for a last look round, noticed that the light was still burning in the house.

"This was very unusual, but since they were awake so late, Davidson thought that he would go up to say that he was in a hurry to be off and to ask that what rattans there were in store should be sent on board with the first sign of dawn.

"He stepped carefully over the shaky planks, not being anxious to get a sprained ankle, and picked his way across the waste ground to the foot of the house ladder.

The house was but a glorified hut on piles, unfenced and lonely.

"Like many a stout man, Davidson is very lightfooted. He climbed the seven steps or so, stepped across the bamboo platform quietly, but what he saw through the doorway stopped him short.

"Four men were sitting by the light of a solitary candle. There was a bottle, a jug and glasses on the table, but they were not engaged in drinking. Two packs of cards were lying there too, but they were not preparing to play. They were talking together in whispers, and remained quite unaware of him. He himself was too astonished to make a sound for some time. The world was still, except for the sibilation of the whispering heads bunched together over the table.

"And Davidson, as I have quoted him to you before, didn't like it. He didn't like it at all.

"The situation ended with a scream proceeding from the dark, interior part of the room. 'O Davy! you've given me a turn.'

"Davidson made out beyond the table Anne's very pale face. She laughed a little hysterically, out of the deep shadows between the gloomy mat walls. 'Ha! ha! ha!'

"The four heads sprang apart at the first sound, and four pairs of eyes became fixed stonily on Davidson. The woman came forward, having little more on her than a loose chintz wrapper and straw slippers on her bare feet. Her head was tied up Malay fashion in a red handkerchief, with a mass of loose hair hanging under it behind. Her professional, gay, European feathers had literally dropped off her in the course of these two years, but a long necklace of amber beads hung round her uncovered neck. It was the only ornament she had left; Bamtz had sold all her poor-enough trinkets during the flight from Saigon - when their association began.

"She came forward, past the table, into the light, with her usual groping gesture of extended arms, as though her soul, poor thing! had gone blind long ago, her white cheeks hollow, her eyes darkly wild, distracted, as Davidson thought. She came on swiftly, grabbed him by the arm, dragged him in. 'It's heaven itself that sends you to-night. My Tony's so bad - come and see him. Come along - do!'

"Davidson submitted. The only one of the men to move was Bamtz, who made as if to get up but dropped back in his chair again. Davidson in passing heard him mutter confusedly something that sounded like 'poor little beggar.'

"The child, lying very flushed in a miserable cot knocked up out of gin-cases, stared at Davidson with wide, drowsy eyes. It was a bad bout of fever clearly. But while Davidson was promising to go on board and fetch some medicines, and generally trying to say reassuring things, he could not help being struck by the extraordinary manner of the woman standing by his side. Gazing with despairing expression down at the cot, she would suddenly throw a quick, startled glance at Davidson and then towards the other room.

"'Yes, my poor girl,' he whispered, interpreting her distraction in his own way, though he had nothing precise in his mind. 'I'm afraid this bodes no good to you. How is it they are here?'

"She seized his forearm and breathed out forcibly: 'No good to me! Oh, no! But what about you! They are after the dollars you have on board.'

"Davidson let out an astonished 'How do they know there are any dollars?'

"She clapped her hands lightly, in distress. 'So it's true! You have them on board? Then look out for yourself.'

"They stood gazing down at the boy in the cot, aware that they might be observed from the other room.

"'We must get him to perspire as soon as possible,' said Davidson in his ordinary voice. 'You'll have to give him hot drink of some kind. I will go on board and bring you a spirit-kettle amongst other things.' And he added under his breath: 'Do they actually mean murder?'

"She made no sign, she had returned to her desolate contemplation of the boy. Davidson thought she had not heard him even, when with an unchanged expression she spoke under her breath.

"'The Frenchman would, in a minute. The others shirk it - unless you resist. He's a devil. He keeps them going. Without him they would have done nothing but talk. I've got chummy with him. What can you do when you are with a man like the fellow I am with now. Bamtz is terrified of them, and they know it. He's in it from funk. Oh, Davy! take your ship away - quick!'

"'Too late,' said Davidson. 'She's on the mud already.'

"If the kid hadn't been in this state I would have run off with him - to you - into the woods - anywhere. Oh, Davy! will he die?' she cried aloud suddenly.

"Davidson met three men in the doorway. They made way for him without actually daring to face his glance. But Bamtz was the only one who looked down with an air of guilt. The big Frenchman had remained lolling in his chair; he kept his stumps in his pockets and addressed Davidson.

"'Isn't it unfortunate about that child! The distress of that woman there upsets me, but I am of no use in the world. I couldn't smooth the sick pillow of my dearest friend. I have no hands. Would you mind sticking one of those cigarettes there into the mouth of a poor, harmless cripple? My nerves want soothing - upon my honour, they do.'

"Davidson complied with his naturally kind smile. As his outward placidity becomes only more pronounced, if possible, the more reason there is for excitement; and as Davidson's eyes, when his wits are hard at work, get very still and as if sleepy, the huge Frenchman might have been justified in concluding that the man there was a mere sheep - a sheep ready for slaughter. With a 'merci bien' he uplifted his huge carcase to reach the light of the candle with his cigarette, and Davidson left the house.

"Going down to the ship and returning, he had time to consider his position. At first he was inclined to believe that these men (Niclaus - the white Nakhoda - was the only one he knew by sight before, besides

Bamtz) were not of the stamp to proceed to extremities. This was partly the reason why he never attempted to take any measures on board. His pacific Kalashes were not to be thought of as against white men. His wretched engineer would have had a fit from fright at the mere idea of any sort of combat. Davidson knew that he would have to depend on himself in this affair if it ever came off.

"Davidson underestimated naturally the driving power of the Frenchman's character and the force of the actuating motive. To that man so hopelessly crippled these dollars were an enormous opportunity. With his share of the robbery he would open another shop in Vladivostok, Haiphong, Manila - somewhere far away.

"Neither did it occur to Davidson, who is a man of courage, if ever there was one, that his psychology was not known to the world at large, and that to this particular lot of ruffians, who judged him by his appearance, he appeared an unsuspicious, inoffensive, soft creature, as he passed again through the room, his hands full of various objects and parcels destined for the sick boy.

"All the four were sitting again round the table. Bamtz not having the pluck to open his mouth, it was Niclaus who, as a collective voice, called out to him thickly to come out soon and join in a drink.

"'I think I'll have to stay some little time in there, to help her look after the boy,' Davidson answered without stopping.

"This was a good thing to say to allay a possible suspicion. And , as it was, Davidson felt he must not stay very long.

"He sat down on an old empty nail-keg near the improvised cot and looked at the child; while Laughing Anne, moving to and fro, preparing the hot drink, giving it to the boy in spoonfuls, or stopping to gaze motionless at the flushed face, whispered disjointed bits of information. She had succeeded in making friends with that French devil. Davy would understand that she knew how to make herself pleasant to a man.

"And Davidson nodded without looking at her.

"The big beast had got to be quite confidential with her. She held his cards for him when they were having a game. Bamtz! Oh! Bamtz in his funk was only too glad to see the Frenchman humoured. And the Frenchman had come to believe that she was a woman who didn't care what she did. That's how it came about they got to talk before her openly. For a long time she could not make out what game they were up to. The new arrivals, not expecting to find a woman with Bamtz, had been very startled and annoyed at first, she explained.

"She busied herself in attending to the boy; and nobody looking into that room would have seen anything suspicious in those two people exchanging murmurs by the sick-bedside.

"'But now they think I am a better man than Bamtz ever was,' she said with a faint laugh.

"The child moaned. She went down on her knees, and, bending low, contemplated him mournfully. Then raising her head, she asked Davidson whether he thought the child would get better. Davidson was sure of it. She murmured sadly: 'Poor kid. There's nothing in life for such as he. Not a dog's chance. But I couldn't let him go, Davy! I couldn't.'

"Davidson felt a profound pity for the child. She laid her hand on his knee and whispered an earnest warning against the Frenchman. Davy must never let him come to close quarters. Naturally Davidson wanted to know the reason, for a man without hands did not strike him as very formidable under any circumstances.

"'Mind you don't let him - that's all,' she insisted anxiously, hesitated, and then confessed that the Frenchman had got her away from the others that afternoon and had ordered her to tie a seven-pound iron weight (out of the set of weights Bamtz used in business) to his right stump. She had to do it for him. She had been afraid of his savage temper. Bamtz was such a craven, and neither of the other men would have cared what happened to her. The Frenchman, however, with many awful threats had warned her not to let the others know what she had done for him. Afterwards he had been trying to cajole her. He had promised her that if she stood by him faithfully in this business he would take her with him to Haiphong or some other place. A poor cripple needed somebody to take care of him - always.

"Davidson asked her again if they really meant mischief. It was, he told me, the hardest thing to believe he had run up against, as yet, in his life. Anne nodded. The Frenchman's heart was set on this robbery. Davy might expect them, about midnight, creeping on board his ship, to steal anyhow - to murder, perhaps. Her voice sounded weary , and her eyes remained fastened on her child.

"And still Davidson could not accept it somehow; his contempt for these men was too great.

"'Look here, Davy,' she said. 'I'll go outside with them when they start, and it will be hard luck if I don't find something to laugh at. They are used to that from me. Laugh or cry - what's the odds. You will be able to hear me on board on this quiet night. Dark it is too. Oh! it's dark, Davy! - it's dark!'

"'Don't you run any risks,' said Davidson. Presently he called her attention to the boy, who, less flushed now, had dropped into a sound sleep. 'Look. He'll be all right.'

"She made as if to snatch the child up to her breast, but restrained herself. Davidson prepared to go. She whispered hurriedly:

"'Mind, Davy! I've told them that you generally sleep aft in the hammock under the awning over the cabin. They have been asking me about your ways and about your ship, too. I told them all I knew. I had to keep in with them. And Bamtz would have told them if I hadn't - you understand?'

"He made a friendly sign and went out. The men about the table (except Bamtz) looked at him. This time it was Fector who spoke. 'Won't you join us in a quiet game, Captain?'

"Davidson said that now the child was better he thought he would go on board and turn in. Fector was the only one of the four whom he had, so to speak, never seen, for he had had a good look at the Frenchman already. He observed Fector's muddy eyes, his mean, bitter mouth. Davidson's contempt for those men rose in his gorge, while his placid smile, his gentle tones and general air of innocence put heart into them. They exchanged meaning glances.

"'We shall be sitting late over the cards,' Fector said in his harsh, low voice.

"'Don't make more noise than you can help.'

"'Oh! we are a quiet lot. And if the invalid shouldn't be so well, she will be sure to send one of us down to call you, so that you may play the doctor again. So don't shoot at sight.'

"'He isn't a shooting man,' struck in Niclaus.

"'I never shoot before making sure there's a reason for it - at any rate,' said Davidson.

"Bamtz let out a sickly snigger. The Frenchman alone got up to make a bow to Davidson's careless nod. His stumps were stuck immovably in his pockets. Davidson understood now the reason.

"He went down to the ship. His wits were working actively, and he was thoroughly angry. He smiled, he says (it must have been the first grim smile of his life), at the thought of the seven-pound weight lashed to the end of the Frenchman's stump. The ruffian had taken that precaution in case of a quarrel that might arise over the division of the spoil. A man with an unsuspected power to deal killing blows could take his own part in a sudden scrimmage round a heap of money, even against adversaries armed with revolvers, especially if he himself started the row.

"'He's ready to face any of his friends with that thing. But he will have no use for it. There will be no occasion to quarrel about these dollars here,' thought Davidson, getting on board quietly. He never paused to look if there was anybody about the decks. As a matter of fact, most of his crew were on shore, and the rest slept, stowed away in dark corners.

"He had his plan, and he went to work methodically.

"He fetched a lot of clothing from below and disposed it in his hammock in such a way as to distend it to the shape of a human body; then he threw over all the light cotton sheet he used to draw over himself when sleeping on deck. Having done this, he loaded his two revolvers and clambered into one of the boats the Sissie carried right aft, swung out on their davits. Then he waited.

"And again the doubt of such a thing happening to him crept into his mind. He was almost ashamed of this ridiculous vigil in a boat. He became bored. And then he became drowsy. The stillness of the black universe wearied him. There was not even the lapping of the water to keep him company, for the tide was out and the Sissie was lying on soft mud. Suddenly in the breathless, soundless, hot night an argus pheasant screamed in the woods across the stream. Davidson started violently, all his senses on the alert at once.

"The candle was still burning in the house. Everything was quiet again, but Davidson felt drowsy no longer. An uneasy premonition of evil oppressed him.

"'Surely I am not afraid,' he argued with himself.

"The silence was like a seal on his ears, and his nervous inward impatience grew intolerable. He commanded himself to keep still. But all the same he was just going to jump out of the boat when a faint ripple on the immensity of silence, a mere tremor in the air, the ghost of a silvery laugh, reached his ears.

"Illusion!

"He kept very still. He had no difficulty now in emulating the stillness of the mouse - a grimly determined mouse. But he could not shake off that premonition of evil unrelated to the mere danger of the situation. Nothing happened. It had been an illusion!

"A curiosity came to him to learn how they would go to work. He wondered and wondered, till the whole thing seemed more absurd than ever.

"He had left the hanging lamp in the cabin burning as usual. It was part of his plan that everything should be as usual. Suddenly in the dim glow of the skylight panes a bulky shadow came up the ladder without a sound, made two steps towards the hammock (it hung right over the skylight), and stood motionless. The Frenchman!

"The minutes began to slip away. Davidson guessed that the Frenchman's part (the poor cripple) was to watch his (Davidson's) slumbers while the others were no doubt in the cabin busy forcing off the lazarette hatch.

" What was the course they meant to pursue once they

got hold of the silver (there were ten cases, and each could be carried easily by two men) nobody can tell now. But so far, Davidson was right. They were in the cabin. He expected to hear the sounds of breaking-in every moment. But the fact was that one of them (perhaps Fector, who had stolen papers out of desks in his time) knew how to pick a lock, and apparently was provided with the tools. Thus while Davidson expected every moment to hear them begin down there, they had the bar off already and two cases actually up in the cabin out of the lazarette.

"In the diffused faint glow of the skylight the Frenchman moved no more than a statue. Davidson could have shot him with the greatest ease - but he was not homicidally inclined. Moreover, he wanted to make sure before opening fire that the others had gone to work. Not hearing the sounds he expected to hear, he felt uncertain whether they all were on board yet.

"While he listened, the Frenchman, whose immobility might have but cloaked an internal struggle; moved forward a pace, then another. Davidson, entranced, watched him advance one leg, withdraw his right stump, the armed one, out of his pocket, and swinging his body to put greater force into the blow, bring the seven-pound weight down on the hammock where the head of the sleeper ought to have been.

"Davidson admitted to me that his hair stirred at the roots then. But for Anne, his unsuspecting head would have been there. The Frenchman's surprise must have been simply overwhelming. He staggered away from the lightly swinging hammock, and before Davidson could make a movement he had vanished, bounding down the ladder to warn and alarm the other fellows.

Joseph Conrad

"Davidson sprang instantly out of the boat, threw up the skylight flap, and had a glimpse of the men down there crouching round the hatch. They looked up scared, and at that moment the Frenchman outside the door bellowed out 'Trahison - trahison!' They bolted out of the cabin, falling over each other and swearing awfully. The shot Davidson let off down the skylight had hit no one; but he ran to the edge of the cabin-top and at once opened fire at the dark shapes rushing about the deck. These shots were returned, and a rapid fusillade burst out, reports and flashes, Davidson dodging behind a ventilator and pulling the trigger till his revolver clicked, and then throwing it down to take the other in his right hand.

"He had been hearing in the din the Frenchman's infuriated yells 'Tuez-le! tuez-le!' above the fierce cursing of the others. But though they fired at him they were only thinking of clearing out. In the flashes of the last shots Davidson saw them scrambling over the rail. That he had hit more than one he was certain. Two different voices had cried out in pain. But apparently none of them were disabled.

"Davidson leaned against the bulwark reloading his revolver without haste. He had not the slightest apprehension of their coming back. On the other hand, he had no intention of pursuing them on shore in the dark. What they were doing he had no idea. Looking to their hurts probably. Not very far from the bank the invisible Frenchman was blaspheming and cursing his associates, his luck, and all the world. He ceased; then with a sudden, vengeful yell, 'It's that woman! - it's that woman that has sold us,' was heard running off in the night.

"Davidson caught his breath in a sudden pang of remorse. He perceived with dismay that the stratagem of his defence had given Anne away. He did not hesitate a moment. It was for him to save her now. He leaped ashore. But even as he landed on the wharf he heard a shrill shriek which pierced his very soul.

"The light was still burning in the house. Davidson, revolver in hand, was making for it when another shriek, away to his left, made him change his direction.

"He changed his direction - but very soon he stopped. It was then that he hesitated in cruel perplexity. He guessed what had happened. The woman had managed to escape from the house in some way, and now was being chased in the open by the infuriated Frenchman. He trusted she would try to run on board for protection.

"All was still around Davidson. Whether she had run on board or not, this silence meant that the Frenchman had lost her in the dark.

"Davidson, relieved, but still very anxious, turned towards the river-side. He had not made two steps in that direction when another shriek burst out behind him, again close to the house.

"He thinks that the Frenchman had lost sight of the poor woman right enough. Then came that period of silence. But the horrible ruffian had not given up his murderous purpose. He reasoned that she would try to steal back to her child, and went to lie in wait for her near the house.

"It must have been something like that. As she entered the light falling about the house-ladder, he had rushed at her too soon, impatient for vengeance. She had let out that second scream of mortal fear when she caught sight of him, and turned to run for life again.

"This time she was making for the river, but not in a straight line. Her shrieks circled about Davidson. He turned on his heels, following the horrible trail of sound in the darkness. He wanted to shout 'This way, Anne! I am here!' but he couldn't. At the horror of this chase, more ghastly in his imagination than if he could have seen it, the perspiration broke out on his forehead, while his throat was as dry as tinder. A last supreme scream was cut short suddenly.

"The silence which ensued was even more dreadful. Davidson felt sick. He tore his feet from the spot and walked straight before him, gripping the revolver and peering into the obscurity fearfully. Suddenly a bulky shape sprang from the ground within a few yards of him and bounded away. Instinctively he fired at it, started to run in pursuit, and stumbled against something soft which threw him down headlong.

"Even as he pitched forward on his head he knew it could be nothing else but Laughing Anne's body. He picked himself up and, remaining on his knees, tried to lift her in his arms. He felt her so limp that he gave it up. She was lying on her face, her long hair scattered on the ground. Some of it was wet. Davidson, feeling about her head, came to a place where the crushed bone gave way under his fingers. But even before that discovery he knew that she was dead. The pursuing Frenchman had flung her down with a kick from behind, and, squatting on her back, was battering in her skull with the weight she herself had fastened to his stump, when the totally unexpected Davidson loomed up in the night and scared him away.

"Davidson, kneeling by the side of that woman done so miserably to death, was overcome by remorse. She had died for him. His manhood was as if stunned. For the first time he felt afraid. He might have been pounced upon in the dark at any moment by the murderer of Laughing Anne. He confesses to the impulse of creeping away from that pitiful corpse on his hands and knees to the refuge of the ship. He even says that he actually began to do so. . .

"One can hardly picture to oneself Davidson crawling away on all fours from the murdered woman - Davidson unmanned and crushed by the idea that she had died for him in a sense. But he could not have gone very far. What stopped him was the thought of the boy, Laughing Anne's child, that (Davidson remembered her very words) would not have a dog's chance.

"This life the woman had left behind her appeared to Davidson's conscience in the light of a sacred trust. He assumed an erect attitude and, quaking inwardly still, turned about and walked towards the house.

"For all his tremors he was very determined; but that smashed skull had affected his imagination, and he felt very defenceless in the darkness, in which he seemed to hear faintly now here, now there, the prowling footsteps of the murderer without hands. But he never faltered in his purpose. He got away with the boy safely after all. The house he found empty. A profound silence encompassed him all the time, except once, just as he got down the ladder with Tony in his arms, when a faint groan reached his ears. It seemed to come from the pitch-black space between the posts on which the house was built, but he did not stop to investigate.

"It's no use telling you in detail how Davidson got on board with the burden Anne's miserably cruel fate had thrust into his arms; how next morning his scared crew, after observing from a distance the state of affairs on board, rejoined with alacrity; how Davidson went ashore and, aided by his engineer (still half dead with fright), rolled up Laughing Anne's body in a cotton sheet and brought it on board for burial at sea later. While busy with this pious task, Davidson, glancing about, perceived a huge heap of white clothes huddled up against the corner-post of the house. That it was the Frenchman lying there he could not doubt. Taking it in connection with the dismal groan he had heard in the night, Davidson is pretty sure that his random shot gave a mortal hurt to the murderer of poor Anne.

"As to the others, Davidson never set eyes on a single one of them. Whether they had concealed themselves in the scared settlement, or bolted into the forest, or were hiding on board Niclaus's prau, which could be seen lying on the mud a hundred yards or so higher up the creek, the fact is that they vanished; and Davidson did not trouble his head about them. He lost no time in getting out of the creek directly the Sissie floated. After steaming some twenty miles clear of the coast, he (in his own words) 'committed the body to the deep.' He did everything himself. He weighted her down with a few fire-bars, he read the service, he lifted the plank, he was the only mourner. And while he was rendering these last services to the dead, the desolation of that life and the atrocious wretchedness of its end cried aloud to his compassion , whispered to him in tones of self-reproach.

"He ought to have handled the warning she had given him in another way. He was convinced now that a simple display of watchfulness would have been enough to restrain that vile and cowardly crew. But the fact was that he had not quite believed that anything would be attempted.

"The body of Laughing Anne having been 'committed to the deep' some twenty miles S.S.W. from Cape Selatan, the task before Davidson was to commit Laughing Anne's child to the care of his wife. And there poor, good Davidson made a fatal move. He didn't want to tell her the whole awful story, since it involved the knowledge of the danger from which he, Davidson, had escaped. And this, too, after he had been laughing at her unreasonable fears only a short time before.

"'I thought that if I told her everything,' Davidson explained to me, 'she would never have a moment's peace while I was away on my trips.'

"He simply stated that the boy was an orphan, the child of some people to whom he, Davidson, was under the greatest obligation, and that he felt morally bound to look after him. Some day he would tell her more, he said, and meantime he trusted in the goodness and warmth of her heart, in her woman's natural compassion.

"He did not know that her heart was about the size of a parched pea, and had the proportional amount of warmth; and that her faculty of compassion was mainly directed to herself. He was only startled and disappointed at the air of cold surprise and the suspicious look with which she received his imperfect tale. But she did not say much. She never had much to say. She was a fool of the silent, hopeless kind.

"What story Davidson's crew thought fit to set afloat in Malay town is neither here nor there. Davidson himself took some of his friends into his confidence, besides giving the full story officially to the Harbour Master.

"The Harbour Master was considerably astonished. He didn't think, however, that a formal complaint should be made to the Dutch Government. They would probably do nothing in the end, after a lot of trouble and correspondence. The robbery had not come off, after all. Those vagabonds could be trusted to go to the devil in their own way. No amount of fuss would bring the poor woman to life again, and the actual murderer had been done justice to by a chance shot from Davidson. Better let the matter drop.

"This was good common sense. But he was impressed.

"'Sounds a terrible affair, Captain Davidson.'

"'Aye, terrible enough,' agreed the remorseful Davidson. But the most terrible thing for him, though he didn't know it yet then, was that his wife's silly brain was slowly coming to the conclusion that Tony was Davidson's child, and that he had invented that lame story to introduce him into her pure home in defiance of decency, of virtue - of her most sacred feelings.

"Davidson was aware of some constraint in his domestic relations. But at the best of times she was not demonstrative; and perhaps that very coldness was part of her charm in the placid Davidson's eyes. Women are loved for all sorts of reasons and even for characteristics which one would think repellent. She was watching him and nursing her suspicions.

"Then, one day, Monkey-faced Ritchie called on that sweet, shy Mrs. Davidson. She had come out under his care, and he considered himself a privileged person - her oldest friend in the tropics. He posed for a great admirer of hers. He was always a great chatterer. He had got hold of the story rather vaguely, and he started chattering on that subject, thinking she knew all about it. And in due course he let out something about Laughing Anne.

"'Laughing Anne,' says Mrs. Davidson with a start. 'What's that?'

Ritchie plunged into circumlocution at once, but she very soon stopped him. 'Is that creature dead?' she asks.

"'I believe so,' stammered Ritchie. 'Your husband says so.'

"'But you don't know for certain?'

"'No! How could I, Mrs. Davidson!'

"'That's all wanted to know,' says she, and goes out of the room.

"When Davidson came home she was ready to go for him, not with common voluble indignation, but as if trickling a stream of cold clear water down his back.

She talked of his base intrigue with a vile woman, of being made a fool of, of the insult to her dignity.

"Davidson begged her to listen to him and told her all the story, thinking that it would move a heart of stone. He tried to make her understand his remorse. She heard him to the end, said 'Indeed!' and turned her back on him.

"'Don't you believe me?' he asked, appalled.

"She didn't say yes or no. All she said was, 'Send that brat away at once.'

"'I can't throw him out into the street,' cried Davidson. 'You don't mean it.'

"'I don't care. There are charitable institutions for such children, I suppose.'

"'That I will never do,' said Davidson.

"'Very well. That's enough for me.'

"Davidson's home after this was like a silent, frozen hell for him. A stupid woman with a sense of grievance is worse than an unchained devil. He sent the boy to the White Fathers in Malacca. This was not a very expensive sort of education, but she could not forgive him for not casting the offensive child away utterly. She worked up her sense of her wifely wrongs and of her injured purity to such a pitch that one day, when poor Davidson was pleading with her to be reasonable and not to make an impossible existence for them both, she turned on him in a chill passion and told him that his very sight was odious to her.

"Davidson, with his scrupulous delicacy of feeling, was not the man to assert his rights over a woman who could not bear the sight of him. He bowed his head; and shortly afterwards arranged for her to go back to her parents. That was exactly what she wanted in her outraged dignity. And then she had always disliked the tropics and had detested secretly the people she had to live amongst as Davidson's wife. She took her pure, sensitive, mean little soul away to Fremantle or somewhere in that direction. And of course the little girl went away with her too. What could poor Davidson have done with a little girl on his hands, even if she had consented to leave her with him - which is unthinkable.

"This is the story that has spoiled Davidson's smile for him - which perhaps it wouldn't have done so thoroughly had he been less of a good fellow."

Hollis ceased. But before we rose from the table I asked him if he knew what had become of Laughing Anne's boy.

He counted carefully the change handed him by the Chinaman waiter, and raised his head.

"Oh! that's the finishing touch. He was a bright, taking little chap, as you know, and the Fathers took very special pains in his bringing up. Davidson expected in his heart to have some comfort out of him. In his placid way he's a man who needs affection. Well, Tony has grown into a fine youth - but there you are! He wants to be a priest; his one dream is to be a missionary. The Fathers assure Davidson that it is a serious vocation. They tell him he has a special disposition for mission work, too. So Laughing Anne's boy will lead a saintly life in China somewhere; he may even become a martyr; but poor Davidson is left out in the cold. He will have to go downhill without a single human affection near him because of these old dollars."

Jan. 1914

Printed in the United States
68764LVS00003B/17